Pagodaville
A Novel
(Book One)

By

Ellen Bennett

Smiling Dog Publications, LLC

DEDICATION

Sandra Moran
(November 7, 2015)

We shall not meet in this world. Your stories, accomplishments, and dedication to good literature are formidable. You left us way too soon. Thank you, wherever you are, for your short but venerable existence.

This is a work of fiction. All characters, locales, and events are either products of the author's imagination or are used fictitiously.

PAGODAVILLE – A NOVEL

Copyright © 2018 by Ellen Bennett.

All rights reserved. No part of this book may be reproduced in any manner whatsoever without written permission from the publisher, save for brief quotations used in critical articles or reviews.

Cover design by Ann McMan

Published by Smiling Dog Publications, LLC

www.smilingdogpublicationsllc.com

ISBN: 978-0-9980277-2-2

First Edition, October, 2018
Second Edition, February, 2019

Printed in the United States of America

ACKNOWLEDGMENTS

Thanks to *you*, the reader*!*

Kris Guay, Editor
I've come to understand the meaning of clunky and cliche. Your educated eye marched right through the mess and cleaned it up. Forever grateful during this first book process.

Diane Long, Editor
I look forward to our continued literary relationship. You and I, we make a good team (on stage and off!).

Suzanne J. Vandersalm.

The following scenario says it all, circa early 2017

-**Me**: Okay, here is chapter two
-**You**: (at kitchen island counter) Oh good! I'm ready.
-**Me**: (I proceed to read) Blah blah blah blah
-**You**: (you get that far-away look in your eyes and your head droops in increments towards the surface of the countertop as I read on)
-**Me**: (continue to read without noticing that you are becoming dangerously over-stimulated) Blah blah blah blah
-**You**: (your head finally lands on your arms at the countertop and the words, "Kill me now" escape from your hidden face)

Thank you for your alert ear, your spot-on transition suggestions, your unending support and love. There isn't anything we can't work out.

Beta Readers:
Kim and Dan Refner, Joyce Dodrill, Rick Ruggles. Thank you for the time and energy you graciously gave towards the project. Your observations and positive energy helped shape the story to where it is now.

Thanks to **Karen D. Badger**. You took the hair-raising task of self-publishing from sheer panic and frustration to *Phew!* The sigh of relief is still felt to this day as I write book two in the same template.

Thanks to **Ann McMan**, author, for being a trusted member of the literary scene, most notably her own wonderful stories, and her recognized expertise with cover design.

Thanks to **Salem West** of *Bywater Books*. Your simple encouragement helped to recalculate the journey of this book.

Cover design: Ann McMan

Author photograph: Fred Western

PROLOGUE
September 1, 1958
Long Island, New York

Vito Carnatelli entered the inner sanctum of the mob boss' home office. He had to let his eyes adjust to the room's darkness, lit only by a small banker's lamp on the desk, before he could approach his boss with the final papers regarding the hit that was to take place in fifteen days.

The boss' face was obscured by a thick haze of cigar smoke from a fat stogie clenched between his teeth. He growled quietly, "You got the results?"

"Yeah." Vito set the papers down in the front of his boss. "Just like you thought, but the last four guys on the list may not have been involved."

The boss took the cigar from his mouth, saliva coating the bitten end. "Hit 'em all. They gotta go. Nobody skims off the family. *Nobody*!"

Vito nodded. He followed orders, was second in command. "Same place?"

"Same place. September fifteenth. Make sure all the trucks are in order. We don't have a lot of time. I'll send the families away for the night. It's the kid's eighteenth birthday so I'll throw him a big party. We gotta work fast on this one."

Vito nodded then turned and exited the office. A whoosh of fresh air slipped in through the open door then settled once the door quietly closed.

The boss lifted his hefty bulk up out of the desk chair and went to the wet bar. He poured himself two fingers of scotch then added ice from a bucket nearby.

A light knock on the door told him it was his wife, Dolores, coming in to give him his evening snack. Every night, at least when he stayed at the mansion, Dolores made him a plate of toast points with caviar and capers, cream cheese, fresh tomatoes, and olives.

He opened the door for her and followed her to the low

table in between two large leather couches, where she set down the tray.

He asked, "This looks delicious. You wanna join, have a drink?"

"No thank you, dear. I'm going to check on Bobby and Georgie. Then I'll call mother. She needs her evening phone call, you know."

He knew Dolores' evening ritual so well. She tucked the boys in, called her mother, then relaxed in a bath of Epsom salts and lavender.

She could feel him more than see him in the dark room. "Are you alright, dear? You seem troubled."

He wanted to tell her how he felt. How hurt and dismayed he was that his own family betrayed him by thinking they could skim off the business. How he was so angry and vengeful, to the point of hitting innocent men. But he diverted his face from hers.

"Just business. You know how it is."

She nodded. She knew very well how it was. It was not her station to question him or inquire into the deeper matters of his business. She knew, because most mob wives knew, that his number, regardless of his position in the family, was going to come up eventually. Not to mention her boys. They too would most likely meet their destiny by design.

But just when and where, she would never be able to calculate.

ONE
Saturday, August 18, 1979
Cleveland, Ohio

The air over Lake Erie was stagnant and heavy. It had been raining on and off for several days and everything from tree branches to ladies' hair-dos drooped in the thick air. Steam rose off the pavement, sun-rays streamed down between broken, angry looking anvil clouds.

Lorna Hughes, Esq., made her way from the taxi cab into the enormous, marble-laden lobby of the Stanhope Building in downtown Cleveland. Her pace had started off strong when she left the comfort of her air-conditioned condominium in Shaker Heights but withered quickly like the weather when she arrived on the seventeenth floor to meet her mother and brothers for the reading of her father's will.

Ever since she was a child, Lorna's relationship with her father had been difficult to navigate. She struggled fiercely to achieve what her brothers were born with: Rights.

Even into her teen years Lorna was still intimated by his very presence. His booming voice, his precise and authoritative actions, the way he moved in the world. She never felt up-to-par with her brothers even though she drove herself fiercely to compete. She strove to win her father's approval, a hug, a nod, his full attention.

All through her formidable years, through junior high school and high school, Lorna kept the fragile parts of herself safe from any scrutiny her father might pass down and focused instead on what she knew he would praise and show her some respect and compassion.

When Lorna graduated with high honors from Case Western Reserve School of Law, her father pulled her aside at her graduation party, sat her down, and looked her square in the eye.

"I always knew you were going to make something of yourself. I am very proud of you. You worked very hard for this. Your whole life, Lorna. I've been watching you your whole life."

Lorna tucked those words close to her heart and never forgot how she felt when he said them, it was more of an honor than her papered livelihood.

It wasn't until Lorna turned thirty that she and her father enjoyed frequent banter about politics, life, current events, and specifically, golf. They were truly father and daughter on the golf course, especially when he would brag to his friends at the Country Club that she was *almost* a better player than he was.

They spoke on the phone or Lorna would go to the house after golf to enjoy a beer or glass of wine on one of the several verandas around the property. She might stay for supper, leaving shortly thereafter when Ellis would retreat to his home office.

Lorna learned that the only way to love her father was to accept him as he was. Never expect more. If only she could be *her* true self with him, the self that fell in love with a girl from high school. The self that held her secrets close to the vest during college, graduate school, and employment years. She vowed she would tell him one day about Jeanie and be strong regardless of his reaction.

But now he was gone.

She would outlive him for many years and already she felt the dull throb of what their relationship could have been had he lived longer.

Her relationship with her mother, Esther, was comfortable. She did not *not* love her, but never really grew to love her *as* a mother.

Lorna regarded Esther as strong willed, bossy. Someone who did not suffer fools lightly and lived unabashedly in a world of money and status.

Lorna's brothers, Gail and Norman, were older by seven and nine years. As kids they got along famously because they were able to stay under the radar and still have fun. As adults, they moved in different circles, spending the requisite time together to appear like a close family, but after the party or get-together, it was usually off to their separate lives. They could go for weeks without speaking to one another.

Lorna never felt alone but at the same time, felt the disjointedness between them. It was just the way they were brought up.

Stand on your own! Don't let 'em see you sweat! Get close, but not too close.

When Lorna stepped off the elevator on the seventeenth floor, she kissed and hugged her mother and brothers then took off her raincoat and unclipped her hair from the back of her head.

"Lorna, when are you going to *style* that mop of hair?" Esther fussed with her own coif now a tangle due to the humidity.

Lorna shook out her dark unruly curls then re-clipped them behind her head. "My hair has been this way for years, mother, give it a rest."

Edgar Seaver, Esq., a gaunt man, emerged from his office to greet his clients. He whistled his 's' and wheezed between words. Lorna thought it ironic that Edgar, a heavy smoker and drinker who probably hadn't brushed his teeth since 1965, outlived her father.

"Esther." He leaned in for a hug that her mother swiftly side-stepped.

"Thank you, Edgar." She nodded then frowned in keeping with the grieving-widow protocol.

Edgar grasped her brothers' hands. "Norman, Gail." They nodded in kind.

"Lorna." He reached for her hand with his paper-thin ones. She squirmed with the feel of his arthritic papery hands.

"So very sorry about all of this." He wheezed. "Shall we go into the office and get started?"

The meeting was long, the legalese wandering. The distribution of funds was to be swift and clean. Lorna had to stealthily pinch herself when Edgar disclosed the amounts in the distribution. She knew her father was worth several million in assets, but his cash stash was unreal. Between she and her brothers, more than a half a million per was revealed. Her mother would be set for life and continue to live in the big family home on Shaker Boulevard.

Her head swam with the numbers.

Instead of going home after the two and half-hour session, Lorna rode the elevator down to the fifteenth floor to her own office where it was bathed in peaceful, ambient light. She tossed her coat and purse on the couch and walked over to her desk chair, swiveled it around to face the windows and sat down.

Her head throbbed.

She reached around to her top drawer, pulled out the aspirin container and shook out two pills. A cup of day-old tea was in reach, so she washed down the pills with the cold, settled liquid.

She grimaced and wiped her lips with a tissue from her pocket, settling her gaze out towards the horizon. Lake Erie tossed gentle waves towards a city beach strewn with rocks and washed up detritus.

She felt hollow, her heartbeat seeming to echo off the large plate-glass windows of her well-deserved corner office. The shock of her father dying so suddenly, so young, caught in her chest. She allowed her tears to flow unabashedly. She cried for her loss, for the empty space that was her father. She cried for herself because despite her large and varied circle of friends, she had no intimate love of her own, someone to hold her during this time of grief.

Her overly-protected, fragile heart never fully recovered from her high school love affair with Jeanie Doyle.

No one had measured up since then.

No one had a chance.

1960's CLEVELAND, OHIO

Lorna met Jeanie in fifth period gym class during their junior year in high school. Lorna typically spent fifth period in study hall but the gym coach, Miss Daisy Horne, Ret. Drill Sergeant from the 31st Division of the Stateside Corp of Women during the second World War, asked her to be her 'wing woman' to "Teach these non-coms how to present on the golf course when they attend corporate functions with their husbands".

Miss Horne had taken a liking to Lorna from the first time Lorna proved her prowess in general gym during her sophomore year.

The day of the class was a warm early spring one with the sun shining high in a cloudless azure-colored sky. Lorna set all the mats with the tees in a straight line on the goal line of the football field while Miss Horne explained the lesson. The girls were to practice their swing first before hitting the ball down towards the fifty-yard line.

Miss Horne then asked Lorna to demonstrate. When Lorna completed her swing and smooth follow-through—the ball heading straight down the line with a beautifully arced intention—Miss Horne, along with the rest of the class, gave Lorna the delicate yet meaningful enthusiastic golf clap.

Miss Horne bounced on the balls of her feet while leaning on her club and addressed the class. "Girls, *that* is how *that* is done." She winked at Lorna and continued to admire her while calling out, "Okay, Lindstrom, you're up."

The attention Miss Horne openly showed Lorna was not lost on the other girls.

In the locker room, Lorna chuckled alongside her classmates.

A sing-song tease: "The old battle-ax has a thing for youuuuu!"

Or "You *know* she is a big lesbian!"

Or "Lorna and Daisy…sitting in a tree…"

And the most frequently asked. "When she gives out the

towels why do we have to be *naked*?"

Lorna took it all in stride, slightly flattered albeit the huge age difference and the fact that Miss Horne truly resembled a warship hit by a Kamikaze.

When it came time for Jeanie Doyle to demonstrate her swing, she started by raising her club high over her head, bending her long legs at the knee while attempting to keep her eye on the ball. She brought the club down as if she were chopping wood and when the club-head hit the mat, the ball slipped lazily off the tee from the resultant thud of the slapping iron. The other girls giggled behind cupped hands. Lorna had to stifle a chuckle as well.

Miss Horne barked out, "Hughes! Help Miss Doyle with her swing so she doesn't shatter her elbows and give us all a big headache with the noise!"

Lorna approached Jeanie and showed her quietly how to hold the club, raise it up and make a clean follow through while the other girls continued with their demonstrations. Lorna took Jeanie through the practice swing several times until she seemed to get it.

When the rest of the girls were done, Miss Horne called out to Jeanie again. Everyone leaned in to watch. Jeanie looked unsure but carried on with dignity.

Lorna held her breath while Jeanie completed the swing.

Miss Horne bounced on the balls of her feet and nodded. "Nice job, Miss Doyle. Thank you, Hughes, for saving me the duty of paperwork from the nursing office."

Jeanie looked Lorna square in the eye and mouthed, "Thank you."

In that moment of eye-to-eye, Lorna felt a sudden seismic shift of the immediate space around them. A collision of color, sound, and air. A palpable spark between two electrical terminals. She had to shake her head slightly to avert her stare. She could feel the same response from Jeanie.

In the locker room, Lorna quickly approached Jeanie before Jeanie had the chance to go to her next class.

"Quite the golf swing there, Miss Doyle." Lorna

playfully bounced on the balls of her feet, imitating Miss Horne.

Jeanie offered up a crooked smile and nodded, "Yeah, well. Golf is *not* one of my strong suits." She added, "Nice interpretation of Miss Horne, by the way."

Lorna chuckled. "Well I think it would be cool to find out what your strong suits are." She had already written her phone number down on a piece of paper. "Let's get together soon?"

Jeanie took the slip of paper. "I would like that. I'm kind of new to the neighborhood. I started school in Fairfax county but we moved last month." She smiled and added, "A girl can't have enough friends, right?"

Lorna nodded.

They began spending time together immediately.

Their senses came alive: The smell right before a rainstorm in a cornfield, the colors of a sunset from the hood of Jeanie's car at the lake, the beautiful architecture of a night sky blanketed in hundreds of tiny lights, the depth of an orchestra performing the work of the masters from Jeanie's hefty classical music record collection.

She and Jeanie found stolen moments at out-of-the-way bookstores where the creaky, slanted, aged wooden floors and shelves full of a variety of books invited them in. They would share their finds under weeping willows or big oak trees in the early summer at the museum arboretum, lazing with Sylvia Plath or Franz Kafka, underlining passages that spoke to them about life.

Their appetite for the passion of discovery was hearty, insatiable. For each new writer or poet or composer or photographer they found, the connection between them deepened.

The first time they kissed, Lorna knew her life would never be the same. Lorna immediately identified with the landscape of Jeanie's lips, their shape, softness and heft. They both felt the deep, intense tug of emotions when kissing each other.

They were sitting on the divan in Jeanie's house in the den. The small television set was on with the volume turned down—a black and white movie that neither of them were really watching— and outside the window the tall trees surrounding the house swayed gently, a sultry windswept odor emanating into the house that can only come in the night.

Lorna had her head on Jeanie's lap. Jeanie traced the curves of Lorna's face gently, her fingers trembling slightly as she passed over the temples, eyebrows, nose and then down to her lips. Then Jeanie leaned down and kissed the lips she had just touched. Lorna lifted her head slightly to meet Jeanie's lips.

Jeanie left Lorna's lips long enough to say, "You take my breath away."

In the months that followed, their need for each other bordered on desperation. If Jeanie was traveling with her family, Lorna could barely contain herself to stay present. If Lorna was traveling away from town, she could scarcely go one day without finding an out-of-the way phone booth to call Jeanie.

It was painful at times for Lorna to be separated from the energy they created together, hard to transition between the fragile, unadulterated love they shared to the stark reality of her life at home and at school.

***

Lorna's phone rang, bringing her back to the present.

"Lorna Hughes," she answered.

"Hey. Where ya been?"

Lorna immediately regretted answering the phone. It was Sally, a recent ex that just *wouldn't* give up. "Oh, hey Sal. I'm kinda busy right now, is this something that can wait?"

Sal hesitated, her voice taking on a slightly wounded tone. "Oh, well, I was just wondering if you weren't busy..."

Lorna closed her eyes. She didn't even want to explain.

"Sal, listen. Let me call *you*, okay?"

"Oh, okay. I was just—"
"I've got to head out now. I'll call you, okay?"

Lorna pressed a button on her phone console to disconnect the call. She knew she was being a bitch, but she had no patience for clingy women.

Sal, like the others before her, never measured up to Lorna's expectations.

Growing Up

Lorna struggled with two personas when she was younger.

The first, and most clearly defined, was the family standard: Get it done efficiently, quickly, and with gusto, show happiness even if you don't feel it, *and* never let 'em see you sweat.

Dinner conversations were more like board meetings, with each sibling reporting on school activities and accolades.

Lorna used her youngest-child status to her advantage. She observed and listened carefully to how her brothers handled their responses, then simply followed suit. Their hard work provided a smooth transition for her to present as the well-adjusted daughter.

Thanksgiving and Christmas holidays at the Hughes mansion were usually big to-do's with hired servers, caterers, and an elite guest list.

The house was appointed by a designer named Lyman Belt.

While most people called people like Lyman a fag or queer or light-in-the-loafers, Lorna admired him because he was so self-assured despite his outwardly feminine mannerisms and vocal inflection.

Her mother accepted his 'happy' personality as "*Whimsical* yet *very* professional! It's what makes him so *grand*!"

Lyman was impeccably groomed and all business. He knew how to work the elite set, to appeal to the wives and convince them they absolutely *needed* his services. Word traveled fast in the upper echelon. Lyman was a household name, a precious commodity of which *every* woman had to have in her cadre of society circle professionals.

Lorna enjoyed watching Lyman work his magic. From her perch on the upper staircase, she'd marvel as he flitted from one end of the vast first floor rooms to the other, his arms full of fabric, plants, or pictures.

She'd giggle behind a cupped hand to her mouth as her zaftig mother tried to keep pace with him, clacking along in her house mules, her lounging attire flowing dramatically behind her, taking notes and calling out approvals or asking questions in his wake.

Lorna loved that Lyman could commandeer Esther in her own house!

Lorna's brothers sometimes joined her on the stairs to watch the transformation before an event, the three of them having spaz attacks when Norman or Gail would imitate Lyman's voice with exaggerated emphasis.

"Let's not *dilly* dally! The seat-covers *have* to go! Honestly, Esther, can we say *housedress*?!" This being said after just a few months of one of Lyman's trendy refits of a particular piece of furniture that was no longer in style.

Into her teens Lorna had the outward appearance of being the girl with everything: Looks, vitality, vivaciousness, brains, a family who was known throughout the city, money, and a wry sense of humor. Boys stood in line to date her. She was intrigued by, but not terribly excited by, the boys, regardless of how cute or popular they were. She liked the convenience of dating, though. It kept an even keel at home on par with all the expectations.

Make-out parties were all the rage. Lorna actually liked watching other girls kiss their boyfriends, imagining herself in place of the boy. She had many girl-crushes but never let on, always observing from a safe distance. Once, while she was kissing Eric Michaels, she looked over his shoulder to watch her current crush, Anne McKay, kiss her boyfriend with passion. When Lorna closed her eyes, it was Anne McKay she was kissing instead of Eric Michaels.

Of course, Eric thought she was totally into him.

Not so much though when he asked her to go upstairs to an empty bedroom and she refused.

But behind the well-rehearsed facade that was her life when around others, she searched for answers as to why she felt a deep, blurry-edged prickling surround her heart at the end of the day.

Thus, the second, more elusive persona.

Lorna enjoyed doing things with her friends well enough, but she flourished best when she was alone. One of her favorite forms of escape was going to the movies. In the low light of the theater when the light from the screen came on, she would allow herself complete immersion and surrender to the illuminated screen.

The Cedar-Lee, in Cleveland Heights, was her movie house of choice. The titles ranged from old black and white classics, foreign films, to independent work that the major theaters did not show. The place was dark, a bit dank and musty, decorated with heavy red brogue curtains, black painted walls with what looked like eighteenth-century gaslight wall sconces. The seats were slightly padded and not very comfortable, but the concession stand offered hot tea and coffee, fresh items from Hough's Bakery down the street, and the best popcorn she ever ate.

Since Lorna's mother rarely inquired as to her whereabouts from junior high school on up, her freedom was unlimited—as long as she continued to present herself as the well- adjusted daughter.

Always, the well- adjusted daughter.

***

Lorna slipped off her shoes, stretched out her stockinged feet on the radiator grill under the window, feeling a calm emptiness. The air-conditioning felt good on her toes, her headache beginning to retreat. Lightening cracked through the clouds, she heard and felt the rumble of the resultant thunder.

Her phone rang again. "Really? *Don't you ever give up?*"

This time she allowed the message machine pick up but when she heard the voice, she grabbed the receiver. It was Avril Klane, her closest friend from their college days.

She smiled when she answered. "Thank God it's you." Lorna stretched the black curly cord around her fingers and swiveled her chair again to face the world fifteen stories below.

"What gives? I tried you at home a million times. Who were *expecting,* anyhow?" Avril said.

"Sal. She already called once."

"Oh gawd, she's such a *noodge!*"

Lorna sighed. "I was just sitting up here watching the storms over the Lake."

Avril's voice softened. "How are you holding up, hon?"

"Well, Ellis was…you know, Ellis." Lorna felt another sob form in the back of her throat. It released quietly.

"Oh. I know sweetie. I'm so sorry." Avril's voice was soothing and gentle.

Lorna grabbed more tissue from her desk. "I've been crying on and off now for…"

Avril attempted an assuage. "Did the meeting go okay? Did your mother behave?" Then added for good measure, "Did Edgar Seaver pass gas?"

Lorna laughed out the rest of her cry. Avril always had good timing.

"Mother was her usual self. Prim and proper, nodding at all the right places, pen in hand. As for Edgar, well, he's just gross, period. I'm sure he slipped a few squeakers in during one of his many hacking fits." She blew her nose again. "Yeah, it went fine. I'm still in shock at how much he left all of us."

"Oh?"

"For me, about eight-hundred thousand in cash and assets."

"Holy *crap*, Lorn! What are you going to do with all that?"

"I don't know yet."

***

Early Summer, 1960's, Cleveland, Ohio

Lorna took a wrong turn while driving towards the Hughes Building downtown to pick something up at her father's office, and ended up on Coventry Road—a long street in a funky neighborhood where head shops, record stores, off-beat clothing, book sellers and an old ratty-looking restaurant called Tommy's-On-Coventry, attracted an array of people Lorna was not used to seeing in such quantity. They were called the *Free Thinkers*, or *Bohemians*.

Lorna's mother insisted they were *all* "Quite questionable in their intentions" and "Not very conscious of their hygiene".

Lorna had no clue how her mother knew all this, but her mother was very well connected and knew almost *everyone.*

But Lorna was immediately enthralled by the gritty, down-to-earth look of the area. She walked up and down the street slowly, marveling in the different types of people milling about or sharing park benches or grassy areas under trees. They were plainly dressed—their style of clothing so different from her spit-shined collegiate mode and penny loafers with dimes in them—and seemed to embrace their environment.

An artist worked with an easel and canvas—her paints and rags spread out around her on cardboard boxes—attempting to capture the scene of people reading, or talking, or daydreaming.

A street performer played a beat-up guitar and sang about how the government was going to—

> *Kill us all*
> *One by one*

In our sleep
So, beware

—in his gruff but in-tune voice reaching out around him. Each time someone tossed nickels or dimes into his open guitar case he smiled and offered a quiet 'thank you' between his lyrics.

Lorna noticed a group of women who were gathered around a blanket in a clearing, tossing a ball back and forth between them. They weren't dressed like the other women she observed—who wore light-fabric skirts and flowing tops with threadbare scarves and funky hats over their long hair—most of the girls that were gathered in the clearing wore t-shirts and cut off shorts or jeans. They looked more like guys. Even their haircuts were short and parted on one side or the other. Some even had a cigarette behind her ear or were smoking. Two of the women had their arms around each other and when they leaned-in to kiss one another, Lorna could not stop staring.

> Two women kissing.
> In broad daylight.
> Without anyone around them saying anything.
> Or seeming to care.

Lorna felt a pulse quicken in her chest, intrigue urging her to watch the group more intently. There was an ease with which these women communicated with each other. They laughed, touched one another openly, and shared raucous conversation.

She left the area that day quite pleased that she had taken a wrong turn in her journey towards downtown.

Coventry quickly became Lorna's tether to her inner-self. She sought out the culture the area had to offer.

Dobama! the community arts theater, hosted several plays a year with local and global talent. She started volunteering at the theater when she was a sophomore in high school. On Friday and Saturday nights she would show the patrons to their seats, hand them a program, the crisp pages smelling of freshly printed glossy paper, then sit in the back row to lose herself in the magic on the stage.

She also ventured to the Cleveland Museum of Art, down the road from the Coventry area near University Circle, where she rambled along from gallery to gallery finding artists that piqued her interest.

On one particular weekend there was a photography show. The work of Berenice Abbott. The show was a collection of Abbott's work for the WPA depicting her vision of New York City.

Lorna spent the entire day there studying each photograph, feeling herself transformed into the compositions. She was intrigued by the grayscale contrast, and how Abbott captured everything from aerial views, to street scenes, to people going about their business in the big city. She went back two more times to study the work.

It wasn't long after the show that Lorna ended up downtown at Fields Camera to buy her first Nikon.

When she learned how to use it, understood the basics regarding light, aperture, film speed, and composition, she carried the camera with her wherever she went, snapping off black and white shots of everything from urban grit to nature. She found she had a good eye for small details. Like a rusty bolt on a busted-up piece of wood in a huge abandoned warehouse, or doors. She loved to photograph doors. Details. She found so much texture and activity in the small details.

On Sundays, she might drive down to the waterfront in Cleveland's Flats area, where blocks of industry surrounded by old warehouses, trains, tracks, and street grime inspired her inquisitive eye.

Or to sit and absorb the quiet, the lack of bustle.

On one such Sunday she found an old cafe with rickety tables on a cement-heaved patio. She ordered a Coca-Cola. The day was hot and humid, and the fizzy, richly flavored ice-cold Coke from the thick green glass was the perfect elixir for her parched throat. While sitting at the rusted table she watched a train rumble through a trestle. She began to count cars, losing track after fifty, or seventy, she wasn't sure. The back and forth cadence of the steel wheels on the track, groaning along the ties, comforted her and made her feel completely independent of her life at home.

Her Sunday forays were her saving grace.

***

Avril interrupted her thoughts bringing her back to the present. "Why don't you come for dinner? Saul went camping with his pals. The kids haven't seen you in a few weeks. Come on! We can order pizza and while the kids get sugar-blasted from too much Coca-Cola. We can sip wine and get slowly smashed! Whaddya say?"

"You're on. What can I bring?"

"Just your lovely self. Oh, hmmm. And maybe ten-grand?" Avril laughed, Lorna laughed.

They hung up.

Lorna replaced the receiver, stood up, straightened-out her skirt and blouse, and felt ready to go back out into the world.

The weather had significantly brightened so she decided to take the transit back to Shaker Square instead of a taxi. The walk to her apartment was just a few blocks from the Square. She picked up a few bottles of wine for dinner and some Halvah for the kids from Binky's Deli.

When she arrived back at her apartment, she turned off the air-conditioner and opened all the windows and slider to her patio. The humidity had dropped, and the air came in fresh and heady with summer blooms. Although the heaviness of her recent loss still surrounded her heart, she felt better than she had felt for several days.

As she undressed and prepared for a shower, Avril's question regarding what she was going to do with her inheritance brought her back to a plan she hatched shortly before her father passed.

1960's, Cleveland, Ohio

As Lorna spent more time in the Coventry area, she listened carefully to the conversations that took place around her, and read articles in the underground newspapers that littered the tables and floor of Tommy's. She began to understand the plight of the underprivileged through the various groups that supported them. She quickly learned first-hand about racial discrimination and the precariously balanced tightrope of the sexual revolution—people getting beaten and arrested for being different. It made her think of Lyman Belt and the women in the park. It made her angry that the mainstream seemed to be careless about these other groups of people. She vowed that at some point in her life she would advocate for them. She didn't know how, but she felt she would.

Lorna's parents made philanthropic donations to politicians, her father explaining that the tax write-off was enormous and good for business. She understood it to a point; however, when she suggested to her mother to explore social groups who really needed the money, Esther claimed that the money was best placed in the political arena.

Why? Because some of the best who's-who parties were thrown for politicians. Ellis Hughes was considering a run for Governor of Ohio.

When it came time for college, Lorna attended Case Western Reserve in undergraduate studies then on to the law school.

When she graduated Summa Cum Laude from Case Western Reserve School of Law, she knew she was on the right track financially to live her own life, support her own desires, and break free from her parents' tunneled vision about the complexities of life beyond their tight circle of reference.

In retrospect, her love relationship with Jeanie only solidified the need for more concentration regarding the homosexual lifestyle and how its presence in everyday life was so under-considered, hidden away and kept quiet.

But during their relationship, Lorna and Jeanie kept their unadulterated love from everyone except their close circle of friends.

They feared scrutiny which would inevitably disturb the fragile balance of what they shared

Lorna was able to live a double life in order to keep Jeanie close to her heart. She knew her other friends would not understand their connection or would ridicule or drop her because of it.

It was so secret, so naively pure.

All Lorna wanted to feel was the safety of Jeanie's heart holding her own.

***

Lorna usually shared her brainstorms with Avril with spritely conversations bringing variables, red herrings, and insights, to light.

Avril, a graduate of Case Western Reserve in Art History had a sharp sense of the world, a hearty sense of humor, and the patience of a saint. She chose to first raise a family before settling into a career—of which she planned to begin after her children were old enough, and her husband was sufficiently ensconced in his own activities in life.

But Lorna did not yet share her most recent idea because she knew Avril would play devil's advocate and play it well

She needed to amass all the information first, in order to convince Avril—and herself—that she wasn't completely out of her mind.

Lorna was on the Board of Directors for the Arts Council of Greater Cleveland. Once a month they invited artists, musicians, and writers to talk about their lives.

After long deliberations, the council typically funded certain projects they thought would benefit both the artist and the community.

During the most recent meeting, Lorna heard a common thread from all the visitors. The money they painfully made from menial jobs went to supplies, rent, and food—in that order. It was such a struggle to succeed, not to mention the endless and suffocating task of paying back student loans.

Lorna understood that choosing a life in the arts was a gamble, no guarantee in sight, a tough go of things until one of two things happened: Success or failure.

Being a patron of the arts and a fellow of the underdog, Lorna fought the council idea of funding a project. While she was unable to convince the council to listen to her ideas about developing an outreach program—something like a 'community-based living situation' with low rent and work space— to help them succeed, she thought seriously about taking matters into her own hands. She didn't want to simply throw money into a fund.

She wanted to *exact* change.

She wanted to start something that would give artists, musicians, and writers a solid foundation from where to work *and* succeed.

She devised a plan but needed to find a location—preferably some place warm, preferably not anywhere near Cleveland—to execute her ideas.

It was time to make a change.

A big change.

She would spearhead a *collective* for lesbian writers, artists, and musicians.

She would find a place where they could live, create, and focus without killing themselves trying to make ends meet. She would offer an environment where they could have a shot at success.

TWO
December 1979
Cleveland, Ohio

Real-estate expert Mort Saunders slid a manila folder towards Lorna, tapping his manicured high-glossed fingernail on it.

He said, "This right here, *this* is the ticket, Miss Hughes. When you informed me that you were looking for someplace out of the way and basic, this popped up just a few days ago from the Florida Real Estate office in Jacksonville."

Lorna studied the information in the folder. He continued to talk while she read.

He said, "It's been on the market for quite some time, though. I think I've found you the real deal."

"When will it be available?"

"Right now! Right this minute! It's been empty for almost a year."

"A paperboy could afford this property. What's the deal here, Mort?"

He cleared his throat. "All I know is that the owner pulled out about a year ago. Something about having to return to Mexico for business."

Lorna asked, "So, the out-buildings are included?"

Mort Saunders nudged the sliding comb-over back up into a clump on the top of his head, holding it there while he nodded. "Yep, everything comes with. The pool, the tennis court, the cabins. All included. Yep, a real beauty, this one."

Lorna studied the black and white photographs of the property. The main building of The Pagoda Motel seemed to be in fairly good shape. The landscaping might have been impressive at one time, but the skeletal remains looked as if a stiff wind might send the parts flying. The out-buildings looked a bit rough, the small oval pool had weeds growing all around it. The tennis court—or whatever the small structure was—sported rusty net poles buried between brush and scrub.

She pointed to it and asked, "What is this?"

He adjusted his glasses, bringing the photograph up close to his eyes. "Well it's too small for a tennis court. Maybe…" he shrugs, "Hmm, not sure. A badminton court?"

"It just looks odd."

"Well, I guess the game was popular back then."

"The place needs a lot of work."

Mort says, "True, but you seem like the kind of gal—uhm—woman who might be able to spruce it up, for certain! The sooner you jump on this the better. We could sign the paperwork and be done with it in a month or two. Just need to set up an inspection and so on."

Lorna wasn't listening as Mort prattled on about how this *would* be *could* be the investment of a life-time.

She was lost in thought. She had the feeling that this run-down property where the sun showed bright and the air was usually clean might just very well be the ticket.

She said with conviction, "I'll buy it."

Two days later, at Lorna and Avril's favorite restaurant down in Little Italy, Lorna finally divulged her plan to Avril.

Avril's eyebrows rose exponentially towards her hairline when Lorna finished telling her about the idea. "What the…and you're *sure* you want to go through with this? A *commune*?"

Lorna corrected her quietly. "A *collective*."

Avril continued as if she hadn't heard Lorna, "I mean, are you having another mid-life crisis, Lorn?"

"No, this is different."

Avril shook her head. "What makes this different?"

Lorna took a sip of her wine. "I feel like I've been living someone else's life. With my father gone, I've had the chance to look at things differently. Like, maybe I don't *have* to live a double life anymore."

"Your dad was pretty proud of your junior partner status, you know. You worked hard to get there. Maybe he would have accepted you more now. But… Are you just going to give up practicing law?"

"Yeah, but…" She sighed then continued. "I'll always

have the law but see, this venture is something I've wanted to do for a long time. And now..." Lorna nodded to no one in particular.

"You'd be giving up everything you've ever known." Avril slipped another piece of pizza off the tray, folding it down the middle, the tip of it just hovering near her mouth. "Well, okay, I'm a little possessive. I don't want you to go." Avril spoke around a mouthful of food. "Oh my God, this is the best pizza in town! Where are you going to find good pizza in down in Schvitzville?"

Lorna chuckled. Schvitzville. She took a hefty bite of her lasagna and then a swallow of wine. "I have no life here. Period." She raised her hand palm-side towards Avril when Avril looked like she was about counter. "And before you tell me that I could have changed things and made a life for myself here, I tried. I know. It just didn't pan out that way. Cleveland has nothing more to offer than lots of memories that haunt me regardless..."

Avril nodded and switched gears after a moment. "So, how come just lesbians?"

Glad for the departure, Lorna relaxed. "Lesbians are still so oppressed. Even in the art world where things are pretty much open and hip. I suppose I could open the door to one and all, but for my money, I think I'm doing the right thing. I can't quite see a collective of straight men and women and lesbians or gay men."

"It's your sandbox."

They ate in silence for a few minutes then Lorna said, "I have been thinking, planning, dreaming, fantasizing, about this venture for quite some time. It *could* work. Maybe I could make a little history, you know?"

"Okay. So, by you buying a broken-down motel in the hottest and most humid state in the country and turning it into a lesbian enclave for artists, musicians, and writers, you are going to make history? Frankly, I think you are making one big-assed mistake."

Lorna leaned in and cocked her head. "Seriously? Did

you *seriously* just say that?"

Avril softened her tone. "Honey, I'm just afraid you're desperate. You know, they say not to make any rash decisions within a year of a parent dying."

"I know, I know. But this is *my* time to move on. I could have done it before dad died but I just…didn't."

"Look, why don't you take the money and go to New York City, or San Francisco where the gay life is abundant? Maybe start a *new* law practice defending gay people? Make a little history that way!"

"Because it doesn't feel like the right move for me."

Avril sat back in her chair, regarding her friend. "Are you sure this isn't some desperate attempt at a lifeboat? Maybe you think if you do this, you'll meet the woman of your dreams, the artist, the musician, the writer, another Jeanie?"

Staring at Avril, her best friend of seventeen years, she saw the depth of care, concern, and maybe even a little bit of fear in her eyes.

But she knew Avril would stand by her no matter what.

She was ready, determined, and had the resources.

"There will *never* be another Jeanie."

THREE
June 1939
Heatherton County, Florida
The Pagoda Motel

Diego Puente heard the old jalopy in the turn-around driveway of the motel. He called out excitedly towards the kitchen that was located behind the office in the main building. "Tita! They are here!"

She hustled out of the kitchen pulling her apron off as she strode. "*Oh, mi dios* I am a mess!"

Diego took her hand. "You always look *bonito*! Come!" He planted a loud kiss on her cheek.

Diego and Tita hollered greetings. They all hugged, so happy to finally be together. Step-sisters Tita and Consuela, arm in arm and speaking excitedly in Spanish, took off towards the main building.

Diego clapped Cesare on the shoulders, looked him in the eye, hugged him again and said, "You are here! We will have such a good business, you and me. *Already* it is good business but now will be *better* with you here. Ah, so *bueno* to see you, *amigo*! I'm so glad you married my sister-in-law!"

Diego and Cesare brought the luggage into the airy lobby. Cesare said, "Oh *amigo*, this is so very nice!"

Tita and Consuela were already in the kitchen picking up where Tita left off making tacos and enchiladas for Sunday supper, chattering, giggling, and singing.

Cesare loosened his tie and took off his sport jacket.

Diego said, "Forget the suit and tie, find your swim trunks and we will go down to the ocean. The water is like a bath today. Come! Tita and Consuela will have supper ready by the time we get back. I have plenty of towels right here!"

"Okay. Well so, should we talk about the business first, though?"

Diego shoved his hands down into his shorts' pockets.

"Ach, you just got here. We will talk about the business later. But now we must go down to the beach and swim! Maybe after supper we will make a bonfire with Consuela and Tita and watch the night stars together?"

Cesare nodded. "Yes, that sounds good, Diego. Sounds good."

When they went out down towards the beach, Cesare noticed that no one else was there. He wondered why, when Diego said the business was so good, the cabins were empty. He thought to ask about it but decided to wait. Diego seemed so excited to see him, he did not want to ruin his first day by asking so many questions.

Later, after supper, they all settled into the soft warm sand, a bonfire crackling up towards a cloudless night.

Cesare listened to the conversation going on around him while watching a jet plane in the distance with its red and green blinking lights as it flew off over the Atlantic Ocean. He sadly remembered a different not-so-nice conversation with his father before he and Consuela were to leave for St. Augustine that very morning.

His father was angry. "You will make big mistakes going to Diego, Cesare."

"But papa, I am ready to live my life with Conseula. There is nothing here but the fields."

His father spat, "And there will be nothing but *problemas* with Diego! The fields have done us well!"

"He is business man, papa."

"He is a cheat!"

"No papa, he doesn't cheat. He makes a good life for Tita and works very hard for people who trust him!"

His father scowled. "*Mafioso!*"

"So what papa? They pay him well, he says nothing, he stays out of trouble."

"And what of Consuela?"

Cesare countered, "Come on papa. If it is dangerous, I would not stay there. We could come back here or go down to Miami with cousin Ricardo."

His father waved him off. "Ach. Ricardo is another one.

Dishonest!"

Cesare knew his arguments would only serve to make matters worse. All he wanted was some type of blessing from him.

After the wedding, his father distanced himself and when it came time to drive off in Cesare's truck, his father hugged Conseula but only nodded towards his son with these parting words spoken in Spanish and in low tones. "If you get into trouble with the *mafioso,* you will not return home."

Diego brought Cesare back to the present. He said, "Look at those stars, will you? So very beautiful."

Cesare and Consuela cooed how lovely the night was, then Cesare said, "I think maybe I am very tired now. The wedding, the drive, it's all so much. In a good way, though." He smiled at his new bride. "Shall we go to bed, 'suela?"

His wife nodded, kissed him on the cheek and stood up. Brushing the sand off of her shorts she took her husband's hand in hers and said softly. "Yes, it is time."

They walked up the path to the motel, leaving Diego and Tita to tend to the ebbing embers.

Cesare woke suddenly during the night when he heard the growling of car engines in the turn-around in front of the main building of the motel. He jumped out of bed and went to the window. Several dark vehicles entered the courtyard and parked on the grass in front of the cabins. The clock next to the bed read five AM.

Consuela joined Cesare at the window. She whispered hoarsely, "Aye, Cesare, *que?"*

Cesare leaned on the windowsill. He watched figures move around in the dark, heard low gravelly voices. A quick chill ran up his spine. He put his arm around his wife. "Come, let us go back to bed."

Later that morning, Diego took Cesare to meet Mister G, the boss. He explained on the way to the cabin, "Now, don't ask any questions. Let me do the talking. They arrived early this morning so Mister G might be tired. Mister G has another property across the mainland. It is called The Palms. He needs people to run that and I suggested to him that you and Consuela would be perfect."

Cesare nodded, confused. He thought he would be at The Pagoda Motel with Diego.

As they approached the cabin, a short heavy-set man with a shock of thick salt and pepper hair and bushy eyebrows over piercing blue eyes met them at the door, a fat cigar jutting from his lips. He wore a white skinny-ribbed undershirt over a large paunch, and his pants were barely held on by an unbuckled black belt.

He stepped out of the cabin and said, "Ah, Diego! Just the man I wanted to see."

Diego bowed slightly. "Good to see you again, Mister G."

Mister G nodded and puffed on his cigar without taking it out of his mouth. He looked at Cesare. "Who's he?"

Diego put his arm around Cesare's shoulder. "This is my brother-in-law, Cesare Alvarez. Cesare, meet Mister G."

Cesare extended his hand and Mister G took it heartily, still puffing on his cigar, the smoke shifting lazily around his head.

Diego said, "Cesare is very excited to have work here. I explained that you thought he and his wife would be good to caretake at The Palms."

Mister G took a longer look at Cesare. "Okay, yeah. I remember that. 'Course!" He asked Cesare, "You have any experience runnin' a joint?"

Cesare stammered, "Well, uh I..."

Diego jumped in. "He is very smart, good with his hands, and learns quickly. In fact, we will start today to teach him and Consuela how to run The Palms. They will do just what we do here, isn't that right Mister G?"

Mister G nodded. "I think we can work things out." He studied Cesare again. "You got kids?"

"Oh, no sir. Not yet."

Mister G nodded.

Diego said, "Mister G, they will wait until they know how to run the motel before they have children. We have already discussed this very important matter." Cesare looked at Diego. They had never discussed this very important matter, at least not with each other.

Mister G nodded again, took his cigar out of his mouth and pointed the ashy end at Diego and Cesare. He said, "Okay Diego. You get all this in order. Teach him good, Diego." He turned around to go back into the cabin and said, with his back to them, "Teach him *real* good."

Diego nodded, "Of course, Mister G. He will learn everything just like you taught me."

The screen door squeaked back on its spring, shutting slightly off plumb. Diego and Cesare stood at the bottom of the steps. Cesare looked at his brother-in-law. He had so many questions, but instead of asking he said, "Okay then Diego, teach me everything I need to know."

A week later Cesare and Consuela knew the drill. They were being paid handsomely to keep their eyes to the ground, their ears deaf, and their mouths shut. Diego taught Consuela how to run the front desk. Tita helped them both with the maintenance of the rooms and property.

When Cesare and Consuela moved into The Palms, they were happy to be on their own. They remained mystified as to the goings-on of their patrons but practiced the laws of their employ, staying out of the way unless needed.

They were anxious to start a family, so they waited a few months until they were comfortable with their duties and had enough money put away to get set on their finances. They redecorated the owner suite, turning one of the smaller rooms into a nursery. Cesare had plenty to do to keep him busy—all the maintenance and upkeep of the grounds—and Consuela was smart and fast on the front desk.

On Halloween of 1939, after a very raucous party at The Palms, Cesare and Consuela cleaned up and went down to the dunes near Heatherton County beach. It was a gorgeous night, the sky full of bright twinkling stars. It was the night they became pregnant.

Consuela gave birth to their first child, a beautiful baby

girl they named Alianah, in July of 1940.

FOUR
Monday March 17, 1980
Heatherton County, Florida

Lorna flew down to Jacksonville, Florida, then rented a car to drive the hour and a half south to Heatherton County to be on hand for the inspection of her newly acquired property.

The ancient drawbridge that connected the mainland of St. Augustine with Heatherton County over the intracoastal waters ended on a paved road with one light swinging overhead. Lorna slammed on the break when the light suddenly turned red. She made a right hand turn with the green light, although it seemed like there was no one around for miles, and followed a small, cockeyed wooden sign with a green arrow that read The Famous Pagoda Motel Turn Left. She headed onto the dirt and gravel turn-around driveway and parked next to a GMC truck that she assumed was the inspector's vehicle.

She felt a surge of excitement because she was finally here. Her first glimpse of the property was a sun-bleached replica of a pagoda listing dangerously to the right, surrounded by a semi-circle of two cement benches in various forms of decay. She imagined the previous owners wanted to exude the feeling of peace and tranquility for their guests, but now it looked more like a war-torn temple and less like the structure of strength and clarity it was supposed to represent.

She turned to look at the front of the main building. Her expectations and short-lived excitement plummeted.

"Oh, my God," she said.

She was met with another sun-scorched wooden structure that might have been lovely at one point in time but now looked like someone had beaten it with a spiked bat. The pictures must have been altered in the darkroom because what she recalled from the realtor was not this. She was afraid to see the cabins. She hoped they were still standing. She heard

Avril's words "one big-assed mistake" echo as she made her way towards the sagging front steps of the building.

"Hello!" A voice came from behind her. A middle-aged man with blue chinos, a white golf shirt, and a great tan approached her. "You must be Mrs. Hughes?"

Lorna corrected, "It's Miss Hughes and yes, that would be me."

He reached out to shake her hand. "Jim Tate. I got here about an hour ago so I thought I would walk around a bit before you arrived."

Lorna shook his hand. "I imagine you have some pretty discouraging news."

"Well, actually, it's not that bad, Miss Hughes."

"Please, call me Lorna."

"Sure. Lorna, it's mostly cosmetic. The whole place, while a bit depressing visually, has pretty good bones. Let's go into the main building here and you can take a look around. It's kind of nice."

Lorna got her hopes up. "My God, I hope so."

Once inside the lobby of the main building, she was impressed with the big wrap-around desk that served as Reception. Beautiful stones and pieces of gray slate were inlaid on the front of the desk in the wood, while the top of was solid redwood. It scarred from use but exuded character. She ran her hand along the molding. "This is stunning. It looks hand tooled."

Jim said, "I think it was. In fact, I believe a good deal of the woodwork here in this building was hand tooled by the initial owners. A Mexican family named Puente."

She looked around at the rest of the lobby area. Wainscoting covered the bottom half of the pale green walls, while areas of darker green where pictures had been hung on the upper part of the walls were apparent. A fan with sagging blades sat at a cocked angle in the middle of the ceiling.

She followed Jim behind the desk into a small office. Carcasses of June bugs littered the floor. She tried to sidestep them but heard an occasional crunch as she walked back into the kitchen.

Lorna entered the kitchen and felt more comfortable. On the yellow walls was a beautifully hand-painted, brilliantly colored—albeit a bit faded—scene of a Mexican gathering where food was abundant on a picnic table, drink bottles spilled out of silver buckets of ice, and children played in a large yard. Black cast-iron pots rested on cement arms over a fire pit.

Lorna remarked, "Oh this is just lovely. It feels so happy and content." She studied it for a few moments with Jim.

He responded in kind. "I agree. It's like a piece of a bigger story, don't you think?"

Lorna nodded. She made a mental note that when it came time to repaint the kitchen, the mural would stay as it was.

Jim opened a cabinet door. "They hang fairly plumb here, see?"

Lorna opened the other doors. "It seems as though the woodwork is very solid. Good workmanship is hard to come by these days."

"You know, my wife and I once thought about buying this place but decided it would be too much work for both of us. We bought a boat instead!" He chuckled. "But I think it's a gem, Lorna. And maybe what looks like a beaten down place now can be fixed up with hard work and creativity, and of course, a bit of cash."

It was at this point that Lorna noticed Jim's gaze fall to her ring-less left hand.

He asked, "Are you just buying the property on your own or will you be joined by someone later on?"

"Divorced. No kids." It was just easier that way.

Jim said, "Oh sure. Sorry to hear. Make a fresh start of things then?"

"Something like that."

They continued up a set of stairs that lead to the owner suite. The master bedroom overlooked the front of the motel driveway. Jim showed her the bathroom. "Full bath and shower, linen closet, vanity, mirror, standard stuff."

Lorna nodded. In her mind, she agreed with Jim that creativity and ingenuity would turn this place into what it must have been like back in the '40's and '50's. Her mind's eye was already tearing the wallpaper down, repainting, and cleaning. More bugs carcasses crunched underfoot. She would get an exterminator first thing.

Jim said, "Why don't we take a look at the cabins? I turned on the water—there is a small unit behind the main building where the water tanks are— but a plumber is going to need to do some basic work."

There were six cabins, three in a semi-circle on each side of a dried grassy courtyard. The pool and tennis court bordered the courtyard area away from the cabins.

Jim said, "The pool is probably not worth fixing. See all those cracks along the bottom and edges? You'd spend a pretty penny fixing it. You might want to fill it in at some point in time. Same thing with this little tennis court thing. I'm not even sure what it is because it's too small to be a tennis court and maybe it's something…"

Lorna offered, "A badminton court?"

Jim nodded, "Yes, you could say that, I suppose. Not sure why they built it, but see here?" He walked over it. "There are heaves all over the place. Dig it up, I say."

Lorna nodded her head. "I've already got some ideas."

They went into each of the cabins and while some of them had two very small bedrooms, all of them had a galley kitchen, a small dining area, a seating/den area and a full bath. She would clear all the old furniture out of the cabins and start over with the basics.

Jim pointed to the windows. "They look pretty good. In fact, I think," he looked through his paperwork, "new windows were installed just two years ago. Yep. Each cabin and the main building were done."

Lorna was hot and uncomfortable in her business/travel attire, hungry, and completely overwhelmed. She asked, "Jim, would you mind if I left you to it? I'd like to check into my motel on the mainland and get something nutritious to eat. The flight was pretty bumpy, so I settled for ginger ale and pretzels."

Jim smiled. "Of course. You run along. Here's my card, come by the office later this afternoon and I can discuss the results with you."

Lorna took his card, shook his hand, and thanked him. She found her way back to her rental car, started the engine, blasted the air conditioning, and stood at the door of the car for one more look at the front of the main building. She was determined to turn this run-down place into a home.

She unbuttoned her suit jacket, took it off and tossed it onto the passenger seat. With a sigh she allowed herself a small smile while looking at the old wooden pagoda baking in the late morning sun. With a grunt, she pushed on the tilted side of the structure to set it back towards center. She held it there and said, "Well, it's you and me now. Shall we make a go of it?"

When she let go of the icon, it stood for a few seconds on its own then slowly creaked its way back to where it originally slumped.

Driving back to the mainland over the intracoastal, the car sufficiently cooled off, she rolled down the driver's side window. The sky was a deep cerulean blue, the calm waters wafted up salty and delicious to her nostrils. She breathed in deep, the air filtering out the Cleveland winter grime from her lungs.

When she arrived at The Palms motel, she found the front desk empty. She dinged the little bell and a short, heavy-set Mexican woman with long jet-black hair tied behind her head and whose smile sported several gold-capped teeth emerged from a back room. "Oh! Good morning, Miss! What brings you to beautiful St. Augustine?"

Lorna set her baggage down. "Well, I'm the new owner of The Pagoda Motel over in Heatherton County."

"Oh *si*! How nice for you! The Pagoda is a little bit of a competition for us here, but I am glad to see it won't stay empty. The more business for you, the more business for me, *comprende*?"

"Yes. I truly believe that."

"And will your husband come to the motel with you as well?"

"Well, actually, ah, no. No husband."

"Oh! No husband. Well…"

Lorna changed the subject. "So, I'd like to check in. I have a reservation for Hughes. Lorna Hughes. And after I get changed, where can a very hungry *single* gal get a good meal around here?"

The clerk's face brightened. "Ah! You must go to El Mocambo. The chef, he is my brother. He will cook for you the best fish you will ever eat. You will tell him I sent you. Each morning he goes to fish!"

Lorna smiled. "And who shall I say sent me?"

The woman continued to speak while she wrote down the reservation information. "I am Cheenah. Okay, here you are, Miss Lorgana Hughes. Room 114. And here is your key."

Lorna picked up her bags and took the key. "It's Lorna, actually. Say, do you know of any good handymen in the neighborhood?"

Cheenah raised her eyebrows and smiled. "My sister, Anya and her husband Milton. They are the Catalvos, and they will work good for you."

Lorna chuckled, "Well, I was looking more for a crew. You know, a few men to do some work."

"Oh no! You don't need big crew. You need Anya. She is crew. She will be the best, really."

Cheenah came around the desk and extended her hand. "I think maybe *I* will take you to lunch at El Mocambo. I will introduce you to the right people at Mocambo!".

Lorna asked, "But…can you just leave? Is there anyone else working here?"

Cheenah smiled. "Just me. Is hokay." She reached behind the desk and pulled up a little sign that read: BE BACK IN UNA HORA, SIESTA!"

Lorna shrugged, liking this woman immediately. "Who am I to argue? I'll change quickly and then we can drive over in my car."

Cheenah shook her head, "We will walk, it is practically right next door!"

Twenty minutes later, Lorna exclaimed when they walked up to the little stucco building, "This is charming, so authentic looking!"

The front patio seating area sported a few wrought-iron chairs and tables balanced on buckled cement. Lorna made a move to sit down but Cheenah directed her inside, where a heavenly scent wafted out of the propped-open door. Lorna could make out a small kitchen, about ten tables, and a neon sign advertising Tecate. Her taste buds tingled in her mouth. She was ravenous.

A tall, gangly young man with a thin mustache, a mop of dark brown hair spilling onto his forehead and a big smile approached them. He wiped his hands on a kitchen towel that hung from the tie of his half-apron. He kissed his sister on both cheeks. "Ah, my Cheenah. You look so beautiful today!"

Cheenah stood up on her tip-toes and kissed her brother on the cheek. She said to Lorna, "He says that I am beautiful *always* even though most times I look a wreck."

Luis waved his hand, "Ach, you will always be *muy bonita*!"

Cheenah wrapped her hand around Lorna's elbow. "Luis, this is Miss Lorgana. She just recently bought The Pagoda Motel. She is new in town!"

Lorna cleared her throat. "Yes, well, it's *Lorna*, actually."

Luis embraced her. "Ah! Welcome Miss Lorgana! Today you will have the house specialty!"

Lorna returned the simple hug gesture somewhat tentatively. She asked, "Okay, what would the house specialty be?"

Cheenah and Luis responded in unison with their forefingers raised. "The fish stew!"

Cheenah waved her brother off. "Go make the food! We will sit."

A young Mexican boy came by the table and dropped off

a basket of freshly made tortilla chips. He set down a white bowl of salsa. Lorna could smell the freshness and dug in.

Cheenah smiled. "You will never get better Mexican food anywhere else, Miss Lorgana."

Lorna shoved more chips in her mouth. "Oh my God." She ordered a beer when the young man returned to the table to drop silverware.

"Miguel, say hello to Miss Lorgana. She just bought The Pagoda Motel."

Lorna went to correct Cheenah again but stopped herself. It was kind of sweet in a slightly annoying way.

Miguel bowed. "Miss Lorgana."

Cheenah leaned in after Miguel went to fetch Lorna her beer. "He is my God son."

"What, are you all related here? You guys must run the town."

Cheenah winked at her but said nothing.

The stew was succulent. Full of potatoes and beans so flavorful between the tartness of the pepper sauce and the sweetness of the fresh fish that Lorna could not speak while she was eating.

Cheenah prattled on about how great the area was and how the tourists came and went. She talked about Anya and Milton and said, "If you want, I will call Anya right *ahora* from the telephone in the kitchen. They work for a man Mister Johnston and he is *el diablo*. Very bad man but they need the work. Maybe they will come and work for you then they won't have to work for Mister Johnston anymore." Cheenah looked at her watch. "Ah yes, right now they are on lunch so they will answer the phone."

Lorna scraped up the last of the stew from her bowl with a tortilla chip. "Well I suppose you could."

Cheenah pushed her chair away from the table. "I will call them, and they will come to The Pagoda after they are done working for that…very bad *hombre!*"

"Okay." Lorna chugged her beer and watched Cheenah walk into the kitchen. She could hear Cheenah and Luis speaking rapidly in Spanish and she was able to make out the words: Anya, Milton, Miss Lorgana, someone named Anita, and Mister Johnston.

When Cheenah sat back down at the table she said, "All is done! I think you are making a smart movement, Miss Lorgana."

Lorna chuckled, "I think the word you want is *move*. Smart *move*."

Cheenah bowed her head and murmured, "Oh *si*. Smart *move*."

"I would like to pay for lunch since you were so kind to—"

Cheenah put her hand on Lorna's forearm, allowing it to linger. "No, no, Miss Lorgana. Today you are *our* guest."

FIVE

After her wonderful lunch with Cheenah at El Mocambo, Lorna took her legal pad and favorite pen with her back to The Pagoda to start her lists.

At three o'clock, while Lorna made notes about the entrance to the main building, a light blue van entered the turn-around and the driver's side door opened as the driver was putting the van into park, sending up a plume of dust.

Lorna watched as a stocky Mexican woman jumped out and adjusted her shorts. Lorna figured this must be Anya, Cheenah's sister.

The closer the woman got, Lorna noticed that even though she looked chunky, she was solid muscle, her arms and legs clearly defined underneath a tight tee shirt and carpenter shorts.

"Miss Lorgana, I am Anya Catalvo, Cheenah's sister."

Lorna smiled and held out her hand. "Hello, Anya. I've heard a lot about you and your husband from Cheenah."

The passenger side door opened, and a thin, small-boned man approached. His tone was gentle and his handshake warm. "I am Milton Catalvo."

Lorna was taken in by Milton's kind eyes. "Hello, Milton. I am Lorna Hughes."

Anya cleared her throat, all business. "Yes, well, right now we can come in tomorrow to see what you need to have done. Cheenah said you needed a crew. We are crew. I will be the handy person and Milton will look at the plants. He is, how do you say, the green finger?"

"Green *thumb* is how it goes. Why don't you and Milton come back tomorrow in the morning. Say, ten o'clock?"

Anya signaled for Milton to get back into the van. "We will not be busy to come at ten o'clock, Miss Lorgana. *Adios*!"

Lorna waved and watched as Anya peeled out of the driveway sending gravel flying up into the wheel wells.

She chuckled and waited for the dust to settle.

Lorna started the rental car and drove to the address on the card for Jim Tate. She found his office in the lovely, quaint downtown square of St. Augustine.

They sat at a small conference table while Jim offered and poured Lorna a glass of iced tea.

She said, "I had the most delicious meal this afternoon at little place called El Mocambo."

Jim nodded. "Ah! Know it well, the food is first rate."

"Good to hear from a native. So, now the bad news?"

Jim went over the specifics of the inspection results. It wasn't as bad as she thought it was going to be. Before she left, he said, "Tomorrow is Taco Tuesday at El Mocambo. You won't want to miss that. Get there early, though, the line is usually down the sidewalk."

Lorna nodded and thanked Jim again for his work.

Taco Tuesday, eh? Maybe she would reciprocate and take Cheenah this time.

Lorna decided to walk around the town before going back to The Palms. The sun was drifting off towards the west and long shadows played against huge trees dripping with Spanish moss, low buildings, and masts jutting up into the early night air from the nearby wharf. She headed down towards the pier. Several pleasure craft were moored to various sized docks. People milled about as boat owners were busy on their decks. Lorna sat down on a park bench, watched and listened to the life around her, allowing the gentle creaks and moans from boat masts shifting in the light surf to lull her into a peaceful bliss.

She knew she could get used to this. From the many trips she had taken throughout her life to exotic islands, this little town of St. Augustine proved to her that exotic didn't necessarily mean perfection. The city of Cleveland, with all its smog and industry, seemed far removed from this lovely hamlet. She felt herself relax even more. Closing her eyes, she listened as the wharf sang a sweet song.

Before Lorna turned in for the night, she dialed Avril.

"Well, hey you! How was your trip down? Fill me in!" Avril said.

"I actually don't even know where to start! What a whirlwind this has been so far."

"Oooh tell me, tell me!"

"Well, first off, the inspection went better than I thought. No major fixes but a freak-load of cosmetic do-overs. Lots of clean up, lots of old stuff."

"Sounds like progress."

"So, the owner of the motel where I am staying, The Palms, is named Cheenah."

"Cheetah?" Avril laughed.

"No, *Cheenah*. Anyhow, she takes me to this amazing little hole-in-the-wall restaurant owned by her brother named Luis, who makes the best fish stew I have ever had in my life and then I tell Cheenah I need a crew to come in and clean up place and make repairs and she tells me her sister named Anya and Anya's husband named Milton will be *the crew.*"

Avril cut her off, cackling. "Oh my God! Stop! This sounds like a freakin' Fellini movie!"

"Av, everything feels so right. I feel like I'm a million miles away from the life I know. Does that make sense?"

"Of course, it does."

"The humidity is pretty intense. I might have to cut my hair."

Avril chuckled. "Sounds like a small price to pay for happiness."

They talked for a few more minutes, then Lorna rang off. She was pleasantly exhausted. She closed her eyes and allowed the thick, sweet smelling night air of northern Florida lull her to sleep. She sighed. "Taco Tuesday…"

SIX
Tuesday, March 18, 1980

When Lorna woke up, she had no idea where she was. It took her a moment or two then she sat up, stretched her long limbs and padded to the bathroom.

After ablutions, she brushed her wavy hair then stuffed it into a clip at the back of her head and looked at herself in the mirror.

She had always seen herself as handsome in a girlish kind of way, thankful that she inherited her fathers chiseled facial features, tall height, and thick black hair. At thirty-five, she was pleased that she looked like she was still in her mid-twenties.

Her love for Jeanie brought out the essence of who she was. Her skin glowed, her hazel eyes sparkled with life, and her smile was all-encompassing. She felt so alive and real with Jeanie, and she wanted *that* rendition of Lorna back.

More than anything, Lorna wanted this new venture to succeed. So far, she had been blessed with everything pretty much falling into place. But a small voice inside kept her quietly vigilant for anything that didn't feel right.

But, so far, so good.

At ten o'clock sharp the Catalvos pulled into the driveway at The Pagoda. Lorna met them outside the main building. Anya jumped out of the driver's seat, clipboard in hand, and said, "Good morning Miss Lorgana. We are *right* on time, *no*?"

"Yes! Perfect! Thank you!"

Milton quietly slid out of the passenger side of the van and went immediately to the leaning pagoda. He ran his hands over the wood then tried to right it. Lorna heard him cluck and speak quietly to himself in Spanish.

Anya said, "I will be back soon. I will go and see what needs to be done."

Lorna attempted to direct her towards the cabins, but Anya was already into the main building and gone from sight. "Okay. Right. Sure."

A police cruiser pulled into the turn-around and came to a stop just a few feet away from where Lorna stood. The driver's side door opened and a tall, blond-haired man, with a thick blond mustache unfolded himself from behind the wheel. He put his cap on and walked towards her.

"Good morning, ma'am. I am Steve Kent from the Heatherton Police Department and I heard you were in town for the inspection. I just wanted to welcome you to the neighborhood."

Lorna relaxed, smiled at him, and approached his outstretched hand with hers. "Hi. I'm Lorna Hughes."

The officer held her hand a little longer than she would have appreciated, and she withdrew it with a little more force than she probably should have.

Steve noticed, nodded, then said, "Everything check out okay with Jim Tate?"

"Boy, word travels fast around here."

He shrugged sheepishly.

She continued. "So far things look pretty doable, just a lot of cosmetic stuff."

"You've certainly got your work cut out for you. I heard the sale price was fairly low."

Lorna nodded. "Yes. But, thankfully, the old owners had the sense to keep things in good order."

He asked, "So you, ah, here on your own or do have some family meeting you?"

"No. No family. Just me."

"We were hoping someone would buy it as an investment."

"Well, in a way it is. It's an investment into my future."

Steve took off his cap and wiped his brow with a handkerchief he grabbed from his back pocket. "Going to be a hot one."

Lorna agreed. "A lot different from up north. It's still pretty chilly and damp."

"Where are you from?"

"Cleveland, Ohio."

"Never been."

"Don't rush."

He chuckled. "Like it that much, do you?"

"Let's just say it's my birthplace and I spent a long time there. It's time to make some changes."

Steve nodded. "I'm born and raised right here in Heatherton County. Small town boy, small town cop. Never really wanted to go anywhere else."

She appreciated his easy way. "I can imagine that."

He put his cap back on his head and said, "Well, welcome to the neighborhood. If you need anything, the station is a mile and half down A1A in Heatherton Township."

Lorna thanked him. "I'm here for just a few more days, and I hope to be on the road from Cleveland within the next four weeks or so."

"Well maybe when you get settled in, I could show you around town, maybe catch a bite to eat?"

"I might just take you up on that, Officer Kent."

He started to get back into his cruiser. "Hey, isn't that the Catalvo's van?"

"As a matter of fact, it is. Do you know them?"

"Oh sure, they're good people. That Anya though, be careful. She's a whip. If she doesn't like something, she lets you know and quick! But she's probably one of the best in town for what she does."

"Oh, and what's that?"

He chuckled. "At being the boss."

He got into his car, started the engine, and backed out of the driveway.

Anya Catalvo came strutting up to Lorna. "Miss Lorgana, I will get my tools. Here is the list of things I must start working on today."

Lorna put her hand up. "Whoa, wait a minute. Slow down there, amiga."

Anya scrunched up her eyebrows. "You speak Spanish?"

Lorna shook her head. "Just a few words here and there. But we have a few things to discuss before you start working on things, don't you think? And aren't you already employed with Mister Johnston?"

"Mister Johnston is no good."

"Well, be that as it may, I wouldn't want you to jeopardize your current job."

"Mister Johnston can go..."

Milton caught up with Anya. "Aye, Anya!" He put his fingers to his lips. He hissed, "*Silencio!*"

Anya scowled at him. "We will work for Miss Lorgana." Then added a bit less forcefully, "If she will have us, that is."

Lorna stepped back. "Okay, hang on a sec Anya. Why don't you give me your list of repairs, and I'll look it over and let you know what I want done first."

Anya handed her the clipboard. "Here Miss. It is in *Spanish* though."

Lorna rolled her eyes and assessed the little Mexican fire-cracker of a woman. "Well, can you at least give me an idea in *English?*"

Anya checked her watch. "Aye, lunch time. We will go to El Mocambo and eat then you tell us what we will do, *si?*"

"Lunch? It's not even eleven-thirty!"

"Have to get there early on Tuesdays. Big crowds come from all over. Come with us now. We will go over and talk about things while we eat. You like El Mocambo, no? Cheenah said you ate the fish stew in three seconds flat."

Lorna countered, "Well, it wasn't *three* seconds per se. It was...oh, what the heck." She shrugged her shoulders and sighed. Officer Kent was right, Anya was the boss. "Okay, you win."

The only mistake Lorna made was allowing Anya to drive. Anya floored the little blue van over the bridge as if she was preparing for take-off. Lorna held on hoping that her view of the bridge would not be her last if the van careened over the edge and into the warm waters of the intracoastal. She let out a breath as Anya thankfully slowed down enough to take a right turn off of the bridge onto Route One on all four wheels.

They arrived just before the big lunch crowd, so they were able to get a table immediately. They were joined by Cheenah and another heavy-set, big-bosomed dark haired and dark eyed woman named Anita, who was Luis' wife. She was serving and hobnobbing with the customers who waited in line.

After dropping off chips and beer at the table, Anita sat down and faced Lorna. "I am Anita. I've heard much about you, Miss Lorgana."

Lorna smiled, not sure from whom Anita heard so much about herself. "Well, nice to meet you, Anita."

"My sister-in-law informs me you will hire her and Milton to work at The Pagoda Motel."

Lorna swallowed a swig of beer. "Well, we really haven't decided on a, ah, uhm."

Anita slapped her large hand on the table, jarring everyone there. "Good! Mister Johnston is a very bad man. He uses us like we are his personal *slaves*! He takes more than half of what Anya and Milton make from the lousy jobs he sends them on. And me," she lowered her voice, everyone leaned in towards the middle of the table to hear her, "he tried to get into my dress one evening, and Luis wanted to kill him that very night! Anya and Milton, they are living with us because they cannot afford a place of their own."

Milton muttered, "Oh Anita, Miss Lorgana doesn't need to know this thing just now."

Anita's eyes went into slits. "She will know soon enough, Milton!"

Lorna wondered if anyone else thought she was still in the room. She said, "Well, I can certainly appreciate all your interest, of course."

Anya set down her now empty beer mug. "Then it's all settled. We will work for Miss Lorgana."

They all looked at Lorna now. She was at a complete loss for words. Nothing seemed quite real, and yet everything made perfect sense. Even when they cut off her sentences and finished them for her, she was certain that these people were going to be significant. She knew that now, before anything got set in stone, she would have to inform them of her plans.

"Listen, I think it would be great to hire you. And you can live in one of the cabins. Maybe be more like caretakers, you know what I mean?"

"Of course, we know what you mean," Anya nodded.

Luis called out from the kitchen, "Order up!"

Anita stood quickly and winked at Lorna. "All will be well, I think."

Lorna waited until Anita was out of ear shot. "But there is one thing you should know about me and my plans for the motel."

Anya leaned back in her chair, narrowing her eyebrows. She mumbled towards Milton without taking her eyes off Lorna. "There is always something, you know?"

Milton urged, "Please talk, Miss Lorgana. We will listen." He sent Anya a glare.

"I am a lesbian and—"

Anya shot forward in her seat and Cheenah stifled a laugh.

Anya whispered, "*Lesbiana?*"

Quietly, "Yes. I am a lesbian." Lorna held her breath and tried to keep her composure while Anya stared her down.

Anya took in a deep breath, looked up in the direction of the kitchen then leaned in towards the middle of the table. "You must not say anything to Anita but Cheenah," she tilted her head towards her sister, "is *lesbiana* too!"

Lorna coughed. "What?"

Cheenah bowed her head, "*Si*, it is true."

Now that Lorna thought about it, Cheenah *was* a tad flirtatious with her yesterday at lunch, but Lorna just figured she was a happy-go-lucky, nice, engaging woman. It explained why, when Cheenah put her hand on top of her arm and kept it there for a few more beats than necessary and she insisted on paying the bill.

"So, *lesbiana. ay caramba.*" Anya rolled her eyes.

Milton shrugged his shoulders. "This is no big deal, Miss. We need to work, and you seem like an honest person."

Lorna thanked Milton for the high mark.

Anya said, "You know, we put extra in the collection plate at church for Cheenah, we can do the same for you, too."

Lorna smiled and shook her head. "Save your money. But there is more to this, still."

Anya's eyebrows went up and Milton glared at her.

"I am going to turn The Pagoda Motel into a collective for lesbian artists, musicians, and writers. I want them to have a place where they can create and learn in a safe environment and maybe even become famous."

Anya asked, "A collection? What is this, a collection?"

"A *collective* is a group of people. In this case, it would be women who happen to be lesbian who are in the arts and want to succeed."

Milton asked, "So, no tourists in and out then?"

"That is correct. I plan on renting the cabins out for long stays. Not like the Palms where tourists come and go."

Anya suddenly stood up and signaled for Milton and Cheenah to join her. "We must think about this, Miss Lorgana. We will come later to the motel." Anya herded them towards the door.

Cheenah squeezed Lorna's shoulder as she passed by her chair. "Don't worry," she whispered.

Anita approached the table with all the food. "*Que?! Donde?!*"

Anya called over her shoulder. "Keep it warm, we will be back later."

Anita set food down for Lorna. "You will stay? I hope everything is okay?"

When Lorna saw the food, she found herself famished and sick at the same time. *What in the hell did I just do?* she thought.

Anita looked quizzically at Lorna. Lorna ordered another beer and said, "Oh yes, everything will be okay."

"Okay, Miss. I don't understand why Anya and Milton *and* Cheenah had to leave at the same time." Anita retreated towards the kitchen shaking her head.

Lorna managed to eat her food. The beer felt good going down. When she paid her bill and went outside, she remembered that Anya had driven, and she would have to hoof it back a mile or so over the bridge.

The afternoon sun hung in the blue sky and the humidity rose. The food, the beer, the conversation sat heavily in her gut for the first twenty minutes of the walk.

She reasoned with herself, weighing everything out in steps: If for some reason Anya decided to tell everyone in town what Lorna proposed to do with motel, she would hold her head high, and if that nice policeman was waiting for her at the motel when she arrived back, she would carry herself as the professional woman she was, be honest with him, and tell him she was going to resell the property!

Yes, everything was going to be okay. She was going to take care of what she had to take care of, go back to Cleveland, re-list the property with Mort Saunders and forget about ridiculous ideas for the rest of her life.

Half-way over the bridge she stopped and looked out over the tranquil intracoastal waters. She leaned her arms on the rail and took in a deep breath. She tilted her head up towards the sun and tried to enjoy the moment before facing the fact that she might have just voluntarily stepped into the end of the story.

The sound of a car horn coming up from behind her jolted her back to reality. She managed to jump back as Anya swerved the van towards the side of the road where Lorna was.

Lorna thought, *Oh my fucking God! She's going to kill me!*

Anya called out from the driver's seat, "We will work for you!"

Milton smiled, his big white teeth gleaming in the afternoon sun. "Yes, we will come work for you, but first we must do other things. We will see you later at The Pagoda."

Lorna sputtered. Relief drained the negative thoughts from her heart, and she leaned back against the rail. "Okay! Okay! Great!" She called out.

Anya peeled off ignoring the other traffic, blaring car horns, swear words and raised fingers.

By the time Lorna arrived back at the motel she was feeling so much better. She sat down on one of the tilted cement benches surrounding the aging pagoda.

She sighed, "Well, looks like it's a go."

Just then a small bird fluttered down and perched on top of the pagoda. It watched her.

She said, "And how are *you* this fine day?"

The bird cocked its head.

"Oh, I'm better now. Thank you for asking!"

The bird looked right at her, chirped, then flew off.

SEVEN
Wednesday March 19, 1980

Lorna gave the Catalvos the cabin closest to the main building. They agreed that they would care-take The Pagoda Motel in exchange for free rent and a monthly stipend with a day off during the week. They had moved a few things into the cabin the day before, but Anya wanted to get in a good cleaning before moving the rest of their belongings over.

Lorna called for a Dumpster first thing in the morning. Most of the cabin furniture needed to go and her plan was to have Anya and Milton begin the declutter process while she was in Cleveland doing her own decluttering.

Then she dialed Avril.

"Are you still picking me up at the airport tomorrow afternoon or should I grab the transit?"

"No, I'll get you. I'll leave the kids with my mom. So, fill me in."

"I hired a Mexican couple to care take the motel. They'll live here in one of the cabins."

"Wow, that was quick."

"I'm trying to trust my instincts."

"I'm surprised. You don't usually do that. Do you know anything about them?"

"No, just the basics. But something tells me they are above board."

"Are you going to put them under contract?"

"I don't think so."

"Whoa, girl, are you okay? What if they up and leave one night, or worse?"

"I don't get the feeling they will. I can't explain it, Avril. There is something about them that makes me feel like this was all meant to fall into place, know what I mean?"

"Yeah, I guess. But for you to take this huge leap of faith…I don't know."

Lorna fidgeted with her toes, running her fingernail over chipped red enamel. "Buying this property *was* a huge leap of faith and moving down here is going to be a huge change. Like I said, I can't explain. It just feels right."

Avril sighed. "Well, okay. You're the boss. I only hope you don't get blindsided."

"Me neither, but if I do, I'll deal with it in stride like I always do. And I'll call you, of course."

There was a brief silence between them.

Avril broke into the dead air. "So, what's on your agenda today?"

Glad for the change in direction, Lorna read her list of things she wanted to do before leaving the following day. "Bank, hardware store, phone company, lumber yard, gardening center. Anywhere I need to set up accounts." She did not, however, mention that she was going to put Anya and Milton's names on the accounts for supplies. She knew she was taking a huge step into the unknown by trusting the Catalvos so quickly.

It was so not like her.

But then again, this whole trip was a journey beyond her comfort zone.

EIGHT
September 15, 1958
The Pagoda Motel

Marco Puente made an innocent mistake on the eve of his eighteenth birthday. He and his beloved Marianna Espinoza were going to have their first conjugal experience together. The plan was to slip away from The Palms where a big party was thrown for him, paid for graciously by Mister G.

The Alvarez and Puente families and friends gathered together. The food, wine, beer, and soft drinks flowed freely. The hired Mariachi band, The Monteverde Brothers, played all night. The guest rooms were 'on the house' so no one would have to go home.

The festive night was in full swing when Marco left the party to get his bicycle, which he had hidden in the bushes prior to the party, for this very moment.

The plan was for him to ride back to The Pagoda Motel fifteen minutes before Marianna was to arrive, so he could get his tiny room 'ready' for their date. They did not want to raise suspicion by disappearing at the same time.

When Marco arrived back at The Pagoda Motel, he witnessed something that would haunt him for the rest of his life.

Marco Puente saw it all.

NINE
June 1980
The Pagoda Motel

It took Lorna five weeks to accomplish her move. When she arrived in mid-May, Anya and Milton, joined by various kin and distant cousins, had begun to restore the property.

Milton and Miguel built another tier and three more legs to give the pagoda a firm structural foundation and balance. Miguel had the task of sanding it down and repainting it, which he did with a high-gloss outdoor weather resistant stain.

Milton and Miguel also pulled every weed, every dead piece of foliage, and replaced them with succulents, hearty blooms, and fresh soil with mulch. Milton installed a new hose system by running various-sized conduit from the main spigot to reach the outer driveway and inner courtyard between the cabins.

Anya, with a tool belt that would make most lesbians envious, clanked around the property fixing plumbing, electrical, and structural issues. With the money Lorna left them for repairs and restoration, they managed to have plenty left over. In Anya, Lorna found a spectacular after-market buyer. Anya knew when and where to get what she needed. She was shrewd and took no guff.

By late June, Lorna felt as though the property was on its way to becoming what she envisioned. Each day at two o'clock, Lorna insisted upon a break from work. The afternoon heat proved relentless and she didn't want to wear Anya and Milton, and herself, out so soon. She made sure she had plenty of iced tea and lemonade in the lobby. They would meet, chat, relax, and then Anya and Milton would retire to their cabin for their afternoon nap. Lorna took the quiet time to read, do paperwork, take a long walk down at the water's edge, or nap as well. She was still getting used to the shift in weather.

Lorna made several changes to the lobby without sacrificing the peaceful, stress-free atmosphere she envisioned. After Anya removed the busted ceiling fan and replaced it with something that looked like it was straight out of Rick's Cafe from the movie *Casablanca*, she designed the rest of the room to keep the dark woods and beige walls in balance. She also replaced the furniture. Not being a huge fan of wicker, she chose instead light weight woods and soft, durable cushions. Glass end-pieces and low elliptical tables made the room cozy yet spacious. She was able to fit her stereo unit in the lobby as well. Continuous music played softly in the background, a soft pop station out of Jacksonville coming in strong and clear.

Lorna stood firm about keeping the mural in the kitchen as it was. The mural, like the pagoda, was part of the initial charm of the old property. It made her feel like she had family even though the family wasn't exactly *hers*. She repainted the areas around it to freshen up the look of the kitchen and even found window dressings to match the colors in the mural. The room flowed, despite the scratched countertops and slightly rusted fixtures.

By the time Lorna's furniture arrived she had painted and cleaned the entire upstairs living quarters. The exterminator made Lorna feel less creeped out by getting into all the closed spaces where the nefarious creatures hid and procreated. She only saw one June bug, red with wings and a determined look in its eye as it flew towards her in the shower, and after using the toilet plunger and muffling her screams into a towel, the bug finally died. The exterminator was on speed-dial on the upstairs phone.

She managed to get Avril's guest room painted and furnished—pink and white like she promised. It was an adorable room. A single bed, small nightstand, dressing table and mirror, and lovely light-weight curtains that shifted in the constant breeze that was northern Florida. Lorna slept in that room for a few nights because it faced the ocean and sound of the surf was just delicious.

The master bathroom was proving a bit harder to get refurbished. Anya and Lorna worked hard to scrape off the wallpaper.

"Jeez, there must be ten layers on these walls!" Lorna peeled off her t-shirt and worked in her bra and gym shorts.

"I know, Miss. Sometimes, you see, when the humidity and condomsation builds up there…"

"*Condomsation?*" Lorna giggled as Anya continued.

"*Si,* you know, like *agua* building up between the layers of the wallpaper."

Lorna shook her head. "I know what you meant, sweetie. The word is *condensation*."

"*Si*! That is what I said, condomsation."

Lorna shook her head. "You're so funny."

"Yeah."

While they worked Anya casually said, "So, you think maybe you and Cheenah…you know…"

Lorna accidentally scraped too hard with her tool and piece of drywall flicked off leaving a good gouge. "Damn it!" Then to Anya, "You know…*what?*"

Anya leaned over and said, "Oh, not to worry, I can fix with the putty. No, I was thinking since you are *lesbiana* and Cheenah is *lesbiana*, maybe you two could get together."

Lorna cut her off. "We are *compadres* and that is *all* and plus the fact, I like my women tall and blue-eyed."

"Well, she isn't the best-looking kumquat on the tree, but she tries hard, Cheenah does," Anya countered.

Lorna thought, *kumquat*? "Has Cheenah ever had a long-term relationship with a woman?"

"Well last year about this time she had many feelings for a white girl. They had a nice "thing" but maybe six months or so the girl left Cheenah to go with a different girlfriend. It was very bad for Cheenah."

Lorna could imagine. She vowed to take Cheenah out to dinner to get the straight dope.

Two days later, Cheenah accepted Lorna's invitation and they ended up at Macs Shack on the wharf where they feasted on oysters, calamari, shrimp, and iced-cold beer from a tap.

Cheenah licked her fingers and said, "*Aye*. This is very good food, you know?"

Lorna agreed while shoving another piece of shrimp into her mouth. "I was so craving this. Glad you like it. Next time let's get lobster."

Cheenah chuckled. "And you know, Miss Lorgana, no one in my family works here either! I think maybe there are other great cooks out there, too, right?"

Lorna laughed. "Sure, but I *still* think Luis is the best, so far."

"Oh, *si*."

Lorna remarked, "It's nice to just hang out with you."

Cheenah said, while cleaning her hands off with a wet-wipe, "You know, I think maybe you and I would be a good sisterhood of criminals."

Lorna had to think about that one for a moment. "Do you mean, partners in crime?" she asked.

"Oh yes! This is what I meant, yes! I think maybe I am *el petardo pequeno* and you are the *mujer caliente*!"

"Translation?"

"Oh, *si*. I am maybe, the little firecracker and you are the hot woman!"

Lorna laughed. "You are the *perfect* partner in crime!"

After dinner they strolled around the marina until the sun slipped off towards the west, sitting lower and lower on the horizon. Lorna felt so peaceful and content, re-connected to life again. Colors popped, sounds became richer, air was easier to breathe even, and she actually *liked* the humidity as it kept her skin moist and rejuvenated.

She sighed. "I love the salt air, don't you?"

Cheenah nodded, "Oh, yes. It is always the best. I remember once I went to the city of New York to make visits. It was cold and very dry in the air. Very hard to keep the nostrils moist, do you know what I mean?"

"Yes, I totally understand. Living in Cleveland was just as bad in the winter time. So darned cold, the wind off Lake Erie. Yuch." Lorna looked over to her friend. "So, Cheenah, have you ever been love?"

Cheenah smiled slightly. "Ohhh. Yes, Miss. I was in love. Once."

"Tell me about it."

"Well, the name of the person I fell in love with was called Elizabeth. She was working down the street from The Palms at the general store. I used to go in there, even sometimes when I really didn't need anything," she nudged Lorna with her elbow and Lorna chuckled. Cheenah continued, "So one evening, I went in and we started to talk. And *boy* did we talk! For many hours after she closed the store. She came over to the motel with me and it like many bombs went off in the sky!"

"ounds wonderful."

"Well, there is not very much to tell, really. We, Elizabeth and myself we lived together over at the motel for about maybe less than a year, and then she just went away. Boom! *Hasta la vista!*"

Lorna felt a tug in her heart. "I am truly sorry, Cheenah. It's never easy when someone you love leaves you."

"Well, she found someone else, you see? Someone else who was not *Mexicana, comprende?*"

Lorna put her hand on Cheenah's shoulder as they walked. "That stinks. Let's go get another beer?"

"Yes, Miss. It really does stinka. I think another beer would be very *bueno* right about now."

On a Friday afternoon just after siesta, Officer Kent pulled into the driveway of the motel. Lorna went out to meet him.

When he unfolded himself from the cruiser he whistled, "Wowza! I don't think I've ever seen this place look so fantastic! When I drove in I thought I was in the wrong driveway!"

"Well, thank you! It's a labor of love, Officer Kent."

"Please, call me Steve." He took off his cap and kept looking around. "Milton Catalvo do all this work?"

"He and his nephew Miguel, actually. Isn't it amazing? Did you see the pagoda?"

He turned and studied it. "Nice, nice job."

Lorna offered, "In the near future I plan on digging up the little court and making the Pagoda Peace Garden. What do you think?"

"I think it's going to be beautiful, Lorna."

"Would you like to see the lobby?"

He moved towards her and followed her into the main building. When he saw it his eyes lit-up. "Holy cow! I can't believe you've done all this work in such a short period of time." He looked around, went up to the reception desk, and ran his hand along the newly sanded and polyurethane surface. "This is just…beautiful."

Lorna was proud of the work she and her team had accomplished so far. "So, what brings you to my door today, Steve?"

"Well, I just wanted to see how things were coming along. I can see that you've turned this place around. And, well I thought maybe now that you're back for good, I could take you to dinner. Do you like Italian food?"

"Love it."

He smiled. "Great! How does your weekend look?"

"I'm always here."

"How about I pick you up at six o'clock on Saturday?"

Lorna felt a tug. Should she talk to Steve now or at dinner? Inform him of her plans and her lifestyle? Her gut belied her instinct to put it off.

She said, "How about we talk for a moment? Would you like some lemonade?"

He looked at her. "Sure. I suppose." He looked at his watch. "I have some time."

"Why don't you make yourself comfortable. I'll be right back."

Steve sat down on the edge of the couch. Lorna went into the kitchen to compose herself. *This could be a disaster.*

When she poured them both a glass of lemonade, she sat down facing him in an opposite chair. "So, I just wanted to talk to you about my plans for the motel."

Steve sipped his drink and nodded. "Okay. You're not going to be running drugs out of here, are you?" he chuckled.

She took in a deep breath and explained. "No, no drugs. A little history here first, okay?"

"Okay, this sounds serious!"

"I am a lawyer, and a philanthropist of sorts. When I lived in Cleveland, I was on the Board of Directors for the Arts Council of Greater Cleveland. We would hear from all types of artists about their lives, their strife in life, their requests for grants, etcetera. I've always been on the side of the struggling artist, musician, or writer because I understand how critical it is for them to be able to live their creative lives without the heavy weights of daily living. Do you know what I mean?"

"Sure. I think so."

"So, Steve." She wiped sweat off the side of her glass of lemonade.

He waited then nodded. "Go on."

"I'm going to rent the cabins out long term to writers, musicians, and artists."

He smiled. "Wow, that's pretty cool. Like a commune?"

"No, nothing like a commune, more like a collective of artists."

He shrugged. "That's different." He sipped his drink.

"There's more." She took a deep breath and just let it flow. "Steve, I'm going to rent only to lesbians."

He cocked his head. "Really." It was more of a statement.

"Steve, I'm a lesbian." She held her breath and waited for Steve to reply.

The look on his face was one of surprise and disappointment. "Okay."

"I know this is a lot for you to take in right now, and uh…"

"Well, I'll admit I'm a bit taken back by this. I'm not quite sure what to say, actually."

"Steve, I wanted to be honest with you right from the get go. Having you find out any other way would be insincere. And I would like us to be friends."

He nodded but said nothing. He scratched his neck, played with his tie, cleared his throat, jangled the ice cubes around in his glass. "Do the Catalvos know about your plans?"

"Yes, I told them right up front as well. It took them a little while to get used to it." She added for levity, "They think if they put more money in the collection plate on Sundays, God might show me the…a different way."

He nodded again, tried to smile, but it came across more like a smirk. He blew out a breath and took another sip of his lemonade. "This is so…"

"I know."

His eyes were not as soft as they were when he came by just fifteen minutes ago. He said, "Well, I'll tell you. Heatherton is a bit like Mayberry. Lots of families with family values. Quiet, friendly. I'm not sure how this is going to wash with the community, Lorna. Most of the queers go down to Lauderdale or Miami."

Lorna bristled. "I get it. I know I'm taking chances, Steve. But first off, the term "queer" is offensive. We are a minority and the harder we push to open the doors to the rest of world, the quicker we can change the language and break down the stereo-types. I'm not looking to open the motel to deviants or people who don't care about their lives. This is a huge lifestyle change for me. You see, my father died earlier this year and, well…"

"Oh, I am so sorry. Was he ill?"

"Sudden heart attack during a meeting. He was the CEO of Hughes Tool and Die Company of Northern Ohio. He was in great shape, never smoked, athletic…"

"Gosh, that's too bad, Lorna."

"So, with a bit of inheritance and most of my own savings, I decided to do something more than donate money to a cause. Give some struggling artists, ones who are serious about their future as an artist, a chance at having a successful journey."

Steve's facial features softened a bit. "You're really serious about this. And hey, I am sorry about being offensive. You're right. The language should probably change." He cleared his throat again. "Well, I have to police the entire county, and you can count on me to be there if you need, it's my civic duty. But again, I can't stop people from reacting however they do."

"Do you think there will be trouble?"

"Hard to say. There isn't a lot of crime here. People just live their lives peacefully. I don't think you'll have Molotov cocktails thrown through your windows kind of trouble. But there might be scuttlebutt and anger thrown your way, or to your tenants."

She reached her hand out to touch his arm, and he involuntarily flinched."It's not catchy."

He sighed and let her rest her hand on his forearm. She rushed to fill in the gaps in conversation. "I'm going to be very selective about who I rent to. The tenants have to be graduates from an accredited school, have references, they have to have a clear vision of where they want to go. I'm not going to charge a lot of rent because the whole idea of rent is to place a value on the living space, but the main goal is to help them achieve a level of success so they can move on, live as they should. Kind of like a halfway point, make or break point."

"It sounds solid, Lorna. I'm impressed with your vision, for sure." He started to get up, "Well, I should hit the road, lots of crime to fight. Thank you for the refreshment."

"Wait, Steve. Don't leave just yet. How about you and I have dinner on Saturday night as planned, as friends?"

He seemed so uncomfortable. "I don't know."

"Look, why don't you sit back down for a moment, okay? I know this is pretty heavy news…"

He sat back down.

Lorna refilled his glass with more lemonade. "Tell me a little about yourself, Steve."

He hesitated. "Why would you want to know about me?"

Lorna pursed her lips. "Come on Steve, let's start this off right. I understand you're shocked, but in time, I hope you'll accept me for who I am."

He looked down at his shoes then back at her. "Okay. Like I said I'm a small-town guy. I married the prom queen right out of high school."

"Were you the prom king?"

He snorted. "Yep. Quarterback for the football team, took us to tournament. I was the guy everyone wanted to be like, the one most likely to get a scholarship to the school of my choice. I was going strong until I tore my ACL and had to have surgery. No more football. So, I got married and became a cop. Then two years later while we talked about starting a family, she met some rich L.A. dude who told her she looked like Marilyn Monroe and should be in the movies, and *bam* off she went. She claimed she had always hated the small-town mentality and didn't really want to be a cop's wife."

"Ouch."

"Yeah, then when I got over that fiasco, I started dating a very nice woman who moved in with me after the fourth date, then after a year she decided she was ready to go back to her ex-husband in Pittsburgh. She never told me she was married in the first place."

"Double ouch."

"And now...you."

She murmured, "Triple play and you're out."

He put his cap back on his head, stood up and headed towards the door. "I should head on out."

"So, dinner on Saturday?"

He hesitated at the door. "Ah, I don't know, Lorna." He started to walk out and she caught up with him. He turned around. "Oh, what the heck. Maybe you can teach me more about the female animal because I seem to be sorely lacking in that department."

Lorna was so relieved she reached up and hugged him.

"Whoa" He awkwardly hugged her back.

"Thank you. Thank you for being a good guy about this.

I know it will take some time, but I'm not letting it go, okay?"

"Well, I have to admit I did *not* see this coming. But I'm a liberal kind of guy. And I like that you are being honest with me." She walked him out to his cruiser. "Still want to pick me up or shall we meet where ever it is you want to go?"

"Either way."

"How about you tell me where it is, and I'll meet you there?"

He gave her directions to Il Capriccio on The Square and climbed into his cruiser. "See you at six then."

"See you, Steve. And, thanks again for being cool."

He semi-saluted her with two fingers to his temple and drove out of the driveway.

Lorna smiled after him, thankful. She was drenched in sweat. She would run down to the ocean in a few minutes to cool off.

Anya approached her looking a bit timid. "What did the *policia* want?" she whispered.

Lorna cocked her head and regarded Anya. "Why, if I didn't know you better, I would say you're a little skittish around the police."

Anya shoved her hands into her back pockets and did not meet Lorna's eye. "Oh, nothing like that, no nothing at all. I was just, you know, curious is all."

"Well he wanted to see the progress, and, we are going out to dinner on Saturday night."

Anya's demeanor brightened. "You mean, a *date*?"

"Not a *date* date. We're going to dinner as *amigos!*"

"Well maybe this little dinner date thing will be good and maybe you and Steve…"

"Annyya!" Lorna waggled her finger at her.

Anya shrugged, giggled, then walked back towards her cabin. "I know you said to keep our money, but maybe Milton and me we *will* put a little extra in the collection plate this Sunday."

Lorna shook her head. She couldn't fault Anya for trying.

Lorna went back into the lobby and the heard the phone ring.

"Hello?" "Hey you! How's everything going?" It was Avril.

Lorna filled her in regarding her conversation with Steve.

"Wow. Big step for you, Lorn. Glad he took it so well. Sounds like you averted a possible freak out by telling him now rather than on what he might have thought was a date."

"Exactly!"

"So, I have a question. What *if* the community down there doesn't accept you or your idea for the motel?"

"It scares the shit out of me, actually. I've tossed and turned many a night going over scenarios. The truth is, Avril, I just don't know. Sometimes I feel maybe I'm not seeing the reality or enormity of what I'm about to undertake. I've been living life in my little protected bubble for so long. Am I being overzealous and blind to the real possibilities that this whole thing might just tank? Maybe. Or am I certain I am going to make changes, one step at a time, and feel safe with those changes? Again, there is no guarantee. It makes me a little crazy, but it's not going to stop me."

"Lorn, it's normal to have these anxieties. It's what keeps you moving forward. Honey, I know you so well. All of this, all the good *and* the unknown, the questions. It's in your blood, you know. You inherited this drive from your father. If I were an artist looking for a soft place to land, I would answer your ad in a heartbeat and move hell and high water to get that motel! Your life has always been about caring for the underdog. Anyone who steps foot in that motel is going to have one hell of a chance at life as an artist."

Lorna thanked her. "So, does this promote me to Saint status?"

Avril chuckled. "Brat. I actually thought my speech was quite stellar."

"It was. It was most convincing. Now, I just have to hope that the potential candidates will see things the way you do."

Saturday night, Lorna met Steve at Il Capriccio at six. They hugged awkwardly in the lobby before being seated.

Lorna said, "I must admit, I'm glad you're here. I thought you might cancel on me."

"The thought crossed my mind. At first, I was feeling sorry for myself because I had hoped for a different type of relationship with you. But hey, here we are," he shrugged.

Steve was still the gentleman. He pulled out Lorna's chair first before sitting down across from her.

A young woman approached the table. "Hi folks! I'm Jillian, I'll be your server this evening."

Both Steve and Lorna looked at her. She was stunning. Tall, light auburn hair tied loosely behind her head, big brown eyes, a lovely smile.

Steve cleared his throat. "Well, hi Jillian. How are you tonight?"

"I'm doing great, how about you two?"

Lorna bobbed her head. It had been a while since someone turned it. "Great."

They ordered drinks and when Jillian moved away from the table, Steve and Lorna eyed each other. Steve's mouth broke into a mischievous grin.

"Stinker," Lorna whispered.

He laughed out loud.

"You know, Steve, I kind of like this. I don't have to be on my best behavior."

The drinks arrived and Steve took a long pull on his frosted mug of beer. "Yep! Me either! Usually when I go out on a first date I get so nervous that I usually end up making an ass out of myself." He licked the foam off of his upper lip.

"I know. My first dates are always weird too. So, I'm glad we're just going to get know one another without all the bullshit, right?"

"Right. So, hey, do you play golf?"

Lorna leaned in to the table. "*Do I play golf?* Oh boy! Let's talk!"

During dinner they discussed sports, what it was like

being a cop, what it was like being a lawyer. By the time dessert rolled around, they opted for a walk on the marina to get ice-cream instead.

Lorna told Steve, "I'll meet you outside. I just want to freshen up."

Once Lorna was in the ladies' room, the door slammed open and in walked Jillian. She approached Lorna in three steps and took her by the shoulders, staring into her eyes. "I've been waiting to do this all night." Then she kissed Lorna passionately on the mouth. She was about to pull Lorna's blouse off over her head when the door opened and an elderly patron entered.

Lorna nodded, "Hello."

"Oh, hello dear." The patron went into the stall and fussed with the lock.

Lorna went back to her deflated fantasy. "One can dream," she murmured.

The other patron said, "Were you talking to me, dear?"

Lorna dried her hands. "No, just thinking out loud. Sorry! Have a nice night."

"Oh, you too."

Steve and Lorna strolled on the marina just as she and Cheenah had done a few nights ago, and stopped at Uncle Izzy's Ice Cream Joint. A storm front was moving in from the west and the air was sulfurous. Heat lightening went from cloud to cloud, making the sky look like it was full of UFOs.

Steve sighed, "Maybe someday I'll buy a boat and head south. See where it takes me."

"Sounds romantic in a solo-kind of way."

He caught a few chocolate chips as they dripped down the side of his cone. He stopped walking and slurped then said, "I think about what you did. Coming down here by yourself on a wing and a prayer, so to speak, not knowing exactly where you would land, or how any of this would play out. It was very brave."

"Well, yeah, the jury is still out. Small steps, brick by brick y' know."

The lightening moved a bit closer.

"How about I walk you back to your car? Looks like we might get a doozy tonight. Heard about the warnings on the two-way."

"Okay. Sure! Let's do this again. I had a nice time, Steve."

"Me too. And a game of golf next weekend? I'm a member at the Heatherton Country Club. You'll be my guest!"

"Deal!"

Lorna was so relaxed and peaceful when she arrived back at the motel that the oncoming storm didn't rattle her. She parked her car and headed to the main building to close the windows and was met with Anya emerging from the bushes.

"Anya! What the…?"

"Oh, Miss. I was just coming up to close the windows. Bad storm coming. Milton is at the cabins right now as we speak."

A brilliant crackle of lightening illuminated the darkening sky.

The thunder shook the driveway underneath their feet.

"*Oh, mi dios!*" They both exclaimed.

Then the birds stopped chirping.

Then the deluge.

Then they *jumped* into the main building.

TEN

Friday, June 20, 1980

The summer heat won. Lorna caved and bought a central air conditioning unit for the main building. The workmen arrived, and in a weeks-time had installed the ductwork, electrical, and the unit itself, with Anya hovering close by to keep an eye on things.

Lorna found relief with the manufactured cool air but still relished the late evening breezes off the ocean. She walked down to the waters' edge almost every night, taking in the expansive sky.

And she made the executive decision to cut her hair. It was getting harder to tame.

She allowed yet another Mexican relative to take care of what Cheenah lovingly named *la pelambrera*—the mop.

"You see, Miss, our cousin Kit is used to working with the thick hair because as you know, we all have the very thick hair like you. Are you sure you're not one of us?" Cheenah giggled. "I think you will like what she will do for you."

And like it, she did. The cut and style opened up her face. Lorna loved the lightness on her head.

Everyone thought she looked *muy bonita*!

Lorna asked Anya to take a few pictures with her Nikon. She made a big show of herself in front of and inside the main building to send to Avril, making sure to include the guest bedroom from several different angles.

When Avril received the package, she dialed Lorna.

"Oh my, God! You look ten years younger! I'm so jealous of your tan! And your green eyes, and the hair cut! The cut is *adorable*! And you're so *buff*!"

"Hi, dearest."

"And holy crap, Lorn! The property looks amazing. I just *love* my pink room! I can't wait to come down."

"Thanks. You can come whenever you want, just let me

know, and I'll come fetch you in Jacksonville. And now, I need your undivided attention to write the ad for *The Lesbian Connection*. I've got so many iterations I don't even know what sounds good anymore!"

Avril said something to one of her children. "Bud! Do *not* flush Barbie down the toilet! *Noooo!*"

"Barbie down the toilet?" Lorna laughed as she tried to picture the scene.

Avril said, "Bud is mad because Lizzy painted red nail polish on GI Joe's private parts." Her voice trailed off, "Bud! I said *no!*" Then to Lorna, "Shit, hang on a sec."

Lorna heard Avril drop the receiver and go after Bud. There was a fracas with Bud crying, Lizzy crying, and Avril trying to calm the masses.

She came back on the phone. "Okay, I'm booking the first flight outta here tonight."

Lorna laughed, "Sounds like you need to, sweetie."

"Honestly, you don't know how lucky you are sometimes to not have kids."

"Oh, you love them no matter what."

Avril sighed. Lorna heard the pop of a wine cork. "Okay, I've got my Zin, I'm calm now."

"Av?"

"Yeah?"

"It's ten in the morning."

"I know. Just a sip. I've already had three cups of coffee and an attempt at eggs with the kids. This is *just* dessert."

They discussed the ad for the next twenty minutes or so. By the time they rang off, Lorna had condensed her version of the ad, as Avril stated it was more like the Cliff Notes for War and Peace, and she was okay with it. She called *The Connection* and was put through to the ad editor, who condensed it even more. It was clean, to-the-point, and gave the proper amount of information. The ad editor thought the concept was a winner. She even joked about giving up her awful job at the paper and writing the next shake-up lesbian novel.

Lorna asked, "So you're a writer?"

"Sort of. I only took two years of undergrad work and got discouraged."

"Oh, that's too bad."

"Yeah, my professors told me I would make a better editor than writer so here I am, editing ads for *The Lesbian Connection*."

"You must meet some interesting people."

"Yeah, if you call meeting them writing their *ads*."

There was a brief silence then Lorna said, "Well, I should get going. Thanks for your help."

"No problem. Good luck with your venture. The paper comes out in two days. Look for it. If you need to reach me, I'm at extension one-oh-eight."

"Thanks." Lorna jotted down the extension.

Now that she had reached this point, she resigned herself to the waiting game. As the ad editor said, it was very unique and it might take a few more ads, perhaps more space on the page, to catch fire.

The ad came out and four days later the phone rang twice. Once it was Lorna's mother calling to check in, and the other call was from Southern Bell to ask Lorna how her service was coming along.

No one called from the paper.

During siesta, while nursing her bruised ego, Anya, Milton, and Cheenah tried to cheer her up.

"Now, Miss. Not to worry."

"Someone will call soon, you'll see."

"It's very beautiful here. It will take a little time."

Lorna appreciated everyone's good tidings but she was felt like something was missing. Maybe the ad should have been longer, more descriptive. She kicked herself for keeping it too lean. She should have listened to her gut and not everyone else. She was not the type to defer so easily.

Just then the siesta was abruptly interrupted by what sounded like several motorcycles arriving in the turn-around in front of the main building. Lorna stood up and went out the front door followed by Anya, Cheenah, and Milton.

They were met by a woman swinging her leg over a large black and silver-chromed Harley Davidson bike.

No one said a word.

The woman took off her skullcap helmet and shook out her shoulder length auburn hair. She wore aviator sunglasses and short black leather gloves on her hands. A black leather sleeveless vest over a white tank top covered her torso, her arms bare, tanned and muscular. Her stance looked to be about five eleven.

Lorna and Cheenah quietly gasped.

The stranger looked at them and cocked her head, "So, is this the welcoming committee or somethin'?"

Lorna blinked her way out of her reverie and approached the stranger. "Oh, I'm sorry. I'm Lorna Hughes. I own the motel. Did you see the ad in *The Lesbian Connection*?"

The stranger regarded Lorna. "Well, yeah. I was havin' breakfast in Lauderdale this morning and since I was headin' up north this way, I thought I'd see what it was all about. I know the ad said to call first so, if ya want I can go to a pay phone and call you then come back, y' know?" The stranger gave a sweet, slightly crooked smile. Lorna pegged her accent as either New York or Boston.

"Of course not! Come on in, we were just having a siesta. You must be parched after your long drive."

Cheenah opened the door for everyone. She looked at Lorna, who brought up the rear. They both whispered, "*Oh, mi dios!*"

The stranger looked around the lobby. "Wow, this is really nice. The cool air feels pretty good. My bike gets pretty hot."

Lorna asked, "Lemonade or iced tea?"

Cheenah nearly fell over everyone to get the stranger two glasses with ice. She poured one glass with tea the other with lemonade. "Is nice to have choices, right, Miss?"

The stranger took off her glasses. Her deep-set, almond shaped eyes were so blue they were almost purple. Lorna stealthily pinched herself to make sure she wasn't dreaming. She looked over at Cheenah who was blotting her brow with a napkin.

"I suppose I should introduce myself." The stranger took a long drink of her lemonade and set the glass down. "Oh man, that is *good*! My name is Doreen. Doreen DiLaRusso. All one word, the DiLaRusso, that is."

Lorna introduced the rest of the family. Doreen pulled off her half-gloves to reveal long luxurious fingers with several silver rings and two thick bands, one on each thumb. Lorna found the whole silver jewelry-against-tanned-skin with short-but-well-manicured nails a total turn-on.

Doreen shook everyone's hands. "Nice to meet ya's."

Doreen offered to Lorna, "See, I'm not really a musician or artist or anything even though I like a lot of different kinds of music and I can appreciate art just as much as the next gal. You're probably wondering why I stopped by."

Who needs a reason when you descended from heaven? "Sure, tell us about yourself."

"Well, see, I'm more of a mechanic."

Anya sat up and regarded Doreen with raised eyebrows. "*Si*. Tell us more, Miss Delrizzo."

Doreen chuckled, "Actually, it's *DiLaRusso*, all one word."

"Oh sure, Miss D. Tell us more about your, ah, *mechanicals*."

Doreen leaned forward, her elbows comfortably on her knees, hands clasped. Lorna tried not to let her gaze fall to the cleavage that presented itself.

"Gimme an engine I can't rebuild. You see that bike out there? I'm the only one who works on it and that's why it runs the way it does." She ran her hand down an imaginary curve. "Smooth as the slope of a perfect butt."

Cheenah gasped. Lorna cleared her throat.

Lorna asked, "So, where are you from originally?"

"Brooklyn."

"What brought you down here?"

Doreen took another long drink from her glass of iced

tea. "Let's just say I had some family issues and needed to come down here and spend some time with my uncle Vinnie."

"Okay. Where does uncle Vinnie live?"

"In Miami. He's kinda like my second dad. My real father died when I was fifteen."

"Oh, so sorry. I know how you feel. My father died earlier this year."

Doreen offered, "Ach, sorry to hear. It's never easy no matter what age, don't you think?"

Lorna nodded. She stared off out a window but snapped back to attention when Doreen continued.

"Well, so anyhow. My family had to relocate because my father followed in *his* father's footsteps, and well, he got bumped off."

Lorna pulled her head back in surprise. "*What?*"

Anya asked, "*Bumped off*? What does this mean?"

"They were in the Mafia."

Anya gasped and nudged Milton, who sat up a little straighter. Cheenah coughed into her hand then said, "So, in the Mafia. Huh?"

Doreen continued. "Yeah." She looked down at her feet. "My mom, my brother, and me were shipped down to Vinnie's pretty quick after dad died. See, Vinnie, he had this big house, a machine shop, a couple of filling stations. His two sons ran the business, and they taught me everything I know. After school I would race home, change clothes, then hang out with boys in the shop. I loved everything about it. So, you could say I learned by hands-on techniques, know what I mean?"

Lorna asked, "What about your brother and mother? Are they still down with Vinnie?"

"My mom moved to Atlanta four years ago with her boyfriend. My brother, well, he thinks he's all tough and everything and tried to be like our father."

"Oh my God, don't tell me he's…"

"Nah. He resulted to, ah, petty theft. Then he decided to

start his own outfit. It didn't do so good, and now he's doin' time in upstate New York."

"Wow. That's quite the story. And you?"

"Never spent any time in prison, if that's what you're asking. No, I'm a regular kind of gal, never really bought into the mob stuff."

Lorna nodded her head, unsure of what to say.

Anya suddenly stood up and motioned for Lorna to join her in the back office. "Oh, Miss Lorgana, I have those receipts you wanted. I almost forgot."

Lorna cocked her head. "Huh?"

Anya put her hand on Lorna's shoulder, squeezed a bit, then addressed Doreen. "Miss D, please excuse us for a moment, we were just discussing these things when you arrived just a little while ago."

Doreen shrugged. "Carry on, ladies!" She picked up the frosty lemonade for a sip.

Once in the back office, Anya whispered fiercely. "That Miss DiLaRazor! I *don like her,* no not *one bit*!"

Lorna studied Anya for a moment. "What's up with you? Why so…?"

Anya cut her off. "I think she might bring trouble is all, Miss. What with all this *mafioso* business, and now her brother!"

Lorna regarded Anya. "Okay. Let's just calm down."

"I know I know. I am just very, how do you say, *protectile* of you, you know?"

Lorna nodded, "Protective. You are and I love it. But let's just see how this plays out. A good mechanic is hard to find." *Especially one who looks like she does. It's not every day that something this exquisite emerges from out of nowhere.*

Anya nodded, "Hokay." She scrunched up her eyebrows and said softly, "But I will keep my eye on this one, Miss."

They rejoined the group. Doreen was regaling Cheenah with Miami stories while Cheenah nodded like one of those head-bobbing statues that people put in the back window of their cars. Milton's eyes drooped in anticipation of his afternoon nap.

Lorna cleared her throat. "Where were we?"

"I was just telling, uh Cheen here, about uncle Vinnie."

"Go on. Don't let us interrupt."

"I lived with Vinnie until I was twenty-one and was able to get my inheritance. I loved motorcycles from a young age, and Vinnie saw how much talent I had in the garage, so he bought me a starter Harley when I was eighteen. My other, uhm, uncles taught me how to take it apart and put it back together again. They bought me all the right tools, and when I turned twenty-two, I found the kit I currently drive now. It's designed for me and for me only. Everything is custom built, custom sized."

Lorna said, "So, you're just kind of a free spirit, then?" *Probably a woman in every port.*

"Yeah, I've been travelin' around for about three years now. I went out to California, hung in Arizona, New Mexico, then made my way back down to southern Florida. Vinnie had to go into the hospital for his liver. Bad liver. We all took turns taking care of him until he got better."

"How is he doing now?"

"He's doing okay. He liked his scotch. Now he just drinks iced tea. Belches all the time. Farts more than usual."

Everyone chuckled.

Lorna had nothing to say. She imagined kissing this beautiful stranger. It was not like her to allow her desires to swell to the surface. She fought them down.

Anya broke the silence and said, "So, Miss. Do you plan to stay around here for very long?"

Doreen looked at Lorna and winked. "Not sure of that."

Anya continued. "So, for instance if you stayed here, and if we have something wrong with one of the vans, or if Miss Lorgana's car breaks down, you can fix?"

"With my eyes closed. And I also fix a lot of other things too. I'm pretty good with any kind of tool."

Lorna thought, *"I bet you are."*

Milton stood up, "Yes, well, speaking of eyes to close, it

is time for siesta nap. Are you coming, Anya?"

Anya stood up and joined her husband. Lorna looked at the clock and said to Cheenah, "Don't you have to be back at The Palms?"

Cheenah's face darkened for a moment. "Uh. Well, yes, I suppose I should go back now. Paula is most certainly pacing wondering where I am to relieve her."

Cheenah took Doreen's hand in both of hers and said, "I hope to see you again, Miss. It was so very nice to meet you."

Doreen stood and bid everyone adieu.

When the lobby was just theirs, Lorna wondered if the air conditioning system had malfunctioned. She was sweating as if she just ran a mile in the afternoon heat. She stood up and said, "Would you like to see the property?"

Doreen nodded. "I thought you'd never ask." She winked. "Lead the way."

When they walked out, Lorna waited for Doreen to join her by her side. Lorna liked the tough guy swagger. It wouldn't work with most women, but with Doreen's mix of feminine and masculine, the swagger was deliciously motivating. "The cabins are around to the back of the lobby this way."

Doreen broke from Lorna's side and walked over towards the little court and pool. Lorna caught up to her and explained, "I'm going to have this court thing excavated, and Milton is going to plant a huge garden around the newly refurbished pagoda. What do you think?"

Doreen bent down onto one knee and picked at the loose surface at the edge of the tennis court. She pulled on a large chunk of blacktop and it came away in her hand with ease. "Sounds like a good plan, Lorna. Kinda crumbly here." Then more to herself, "Wonder what's underneath it."

Lorna did not hear the last part, as she was already walking towards the pool. "Yes. And I'll probably fill this in."

Doreen looked at the court for another few moments then rose to meet Lorna at the empty pool edge. "Another good plan. Very cracked and probably unsafe." Doreen wondered what was buried under *it*.

"Not to mention plain ugly," Lorna added.

"Yeah, well, there's that. Hey, your ad said the dunes are a stones-throw away from the cabins. How 'bout we head down there?"

"Well, don't you want to see the cabins?"

"Nah, let's do that later. This is the perfect time to swim."

"Well, I can run in and get us some towels and change into my bathing suit."

Doreen grabbed Lorna's hand. "C'mon, let's just go down there!"

Keep holding my hand and I'll run along-side of your motorcycle. On the highway. Well, probably not the highway. She hesitated for a moment then said, "Okay. Sure, why not?"

"Lead the way!"

They walked down to the dunes hand in hand and for some reason this did not bother Lorna. It felt good to touch another woman, one that she was so physically attracted to. *Jeez it hasn't even been an hour*!

Doreen sighed when they got to the top of a dune. "I never get tired of the ocean, know what I mean?"

Lorna nodded. "Didn't get too much of that in Arizona or New Mexico, did you?"

"Oh hey, check it out! There's a great log down there!"

Doreen slid down the dune. She pulled off her boots, then her socks.

Lorna hung back for a moment.

"C'mon!" Doreen had already pulled off her jeans which revealed black bikini underwear over what Lorna could only imagine was certain to be sexy as hell. Doreen's long legs strode her towards the log. When she got there, she rolled up her jeans, tossed the lump down against the log to use as a headrest and plopped down in the sand.

Lorna caught up with her. She surveyed the beach, thankful that they were the only ones there. When she turned back to face Doreen, Doreen had pulled off her tank top. Lorna's breath caught in her throat. Doreen had perfect smallish breasts tanned just as evenly as the rest of her body.

"Oh, this sun!" She pulled up her aviators to the top of her head. "Don't want to get weird tan lines."

Lorna sat down next to Doreen and pulled her legs up towards her chest. If she were a poet she would conjure up every metaphor she could to explain Doreen's body. If she were an artist, she would pull every possible media available to cast Doreen's body in a timeless portrayal. A bead of sweat traveled down Doreen's chin and neck and pooled in the notch right above the breastbone. Lorna fought the desire to lean over and taste her.

Doreen asked Lorna, "So, tell me about yourself, Lorna Hughes."

Lorna stretched out her legs and leaned back onto her elbows, thankful for the break. The sand was hot and she regretted not bringing a towel down. She thought it was so odd to chit-chat with a perfect stranger who was practically naked. This was a new one for her.

"Well, I was born and raised in Cleveland, Ohio. Went to law school, practiced for ten years, needed a change in my life, and here I am."

Doreen chuckled, "Right to the point, eh Counselor?"

"It's one of those things, where do I start, you know?"

"Well, how about why you decided to come down here and start this motel thing?"

"It goes back a way. When I lived in Cleveland, I was on the Board of Directors for Arts Council of Greater Cleveland. I met some great people, students, struggling artists, folks who had to fight their way through life to achieve a modicum of success."

"Kind of like the starving artist thing, right?"

"Right. And starving they were. The council appropriated funds for various grants and associations to help the artist live and eat while honing their craft. And since I was bored to tears and fed up with the Cleveland lifestyle, not to mention the weather, I decided to do something more for my fellow womankind. Thus, The Pagoda Motel. A clean start, a fresh outlook on life."

"A very brave move, Lorna. I respect a gal who knows what she wants. How old are you?"

"Actually, I'll be thirty-six in October."

"It's never too late to start over."

Lorna shifted. She was sweating.

Doreen shaded her eyes and looked up at Lorna. "Why don't you take off your t-shirt and shorts. You look pretty hot."

Lorna thought about it. She was melting. What would the big deal be? Bra and panties, like a two-piece. She thanked herself for putting matching under garments on this morning. She stripped down while Doreen continued to shade her eyes and watch.

"You look pretty dang good for thirty-five."

Lorna playfully slugged Doreen's shoulder, "Well for God's sake I'm not over the freakin' hill yet. How old are *you*?"

Doreen laughed. "I get asked that all the time. My cousins tell me I still act like a sixteen -year -old. I'm twenty-eight."

"So, I'm not old enough to be your mother and still young enough to look good without clothes on."

Doreen surveyed Lorna's body. "Yep, I'd agree." Doreen looked into Lorna's eyes.

Lorna regarded Doreen. "You're such a free-spirit. Were you always so comfortable in your own skin?"

"Not always, Lorna. I'd have to say it was pretty tough growing up. But Vinnie made me feel so, I dunno, independent. Like, no one could get in my face, know what I mean?"

Lorna nodded. "Sure." She wondered if the tough-guy act covered up rock hard emotions stuffed away into little compartments.

Doreen suddenly shot up from her supine position. "Damn its hot! Last one in's a rotten egg." She dashed off towards the water's edge.

Lorna sat there for a moment, stunned.

Doreen called out, "C'mon in, the water is amazing!"

Lorna jogged down to meet her.

Once in the water, they swam out a bit but still close enough to stand. Doreen turned to face Lorna and Lorna fell head-over-heels into the deep-set blue-purple eyes of this glorious woman. Doreen took Lorna by the shoulders and kissed her on the mouth.

Lorna, too shocked to respond immediately, looked at Doreen then said, "Oh, my God."

"How was that?"

Lorna said nothing. Her gut spoke for her. *Kiss her back. Give in to the years of malaise.*

She felt a power surge release itself throughout her body. She reached over to Doreen, gently grabbed her by her wet hair, and pulled her face towards hers for another kiss. Doreen's lips were soft yet firm.

Doreen deftly unhooked Lorna's bra and pulled it over her arms. It landed in the water and started to float away. Then, she slipped Lorna's underwear off. Those too, rose to the top of the water and floated lazily away.

Lorna wrapped her legs around Doreen's waist as if her body was a magnet to Doreen's steel. She felt a flash-fire spread throughout her belly and into her groin. Soon the two were intertwined, kissing, touching, probing, moaning, nibbling on wet necks, running hands through wet hair. Every time Lorna opened her eyes to look at Doreen, she felt the draw suck her back in.

"You are so beautiful."

"I just want to crawl all over you.

"Hold me close."

"This is so crazy."

"When I first saw you…"

"Don't hold back."

"Your mouth…I just want to…"

"Keep kissing me."

"I need you inside me."

Then Doreen entered her. Lorna quickly understood the value of the thumb rings. The feel of the soft polished silver against her was unstoppable. Lorna had an orgasm faster than she ever thought she could, it was pure animal need now. She had another one almost as quickly. She held onto Doreen's waist for dear life. Doreen held her steady and strong.

And then, the dam broke.

Lorna felt the swell start deep in her belly and work its way up through her midsection and into her throat. She started to shake and cry. She had no control over this one. She clung to Doreen as if the thickness of Doreen's body would shield her from whatever was erupting from her depths.

Doreen whispered, "Hey now. Hey, you okay?"

Lorna continued to cry, she couldn't talk. Sobs racked her whole body.

"Easy does it, babe." Doreen cooed, moving strands of wet hair off of Lorna's face.

Lorna had a moment of lucidness and detached herself from Doreen's waist. She shrilled. "Babe? *Babe?* Is *that* what this was? Another *conquest?* Do you do this with *all* the *babes* you meet?"

"Whoa, whoa! Lorna, what the heck?" Doreen's eyes went from soft to guarded.

Lorna pushed herself away from Doreen. "Just get your clothes, get on your *hog* and leave here!"

"But, wait a minute! You wanted this as much as I did." Doreen's face changed from guarded to hard and pointy.

Lorna's eyes were so blurred from her tears that all she was able to do was gut react. "Just go!"

Doreen stood stock still for a moment. "Uhm, a little blind-sided here, Lorna. What happened?"

Lorna turned her back to Doreen and wrapped her arms around her exposed chest. "Who do you think you are? Showing up at my door..." She hugged herself and shook. The sun-drenched water losing its warmth.

"Lorna, it...c'mon, we were just having fun. It all seemed so natural."

Lorna couldn't stop the thrust of her emotions. Her chest filled with forced air. She croaked out, "Just go."

Doreen muttered, "This is ridiculous." And made her way out of the water.

When Doreen got back to the log, she grabbed her clothes and tried to put them on. She managed to get her tank top half-way back on, then staggered as she pulled at her jeans. "This is so fucked up."

She dried and cleaned her feet off with her socks, pulled her boots on and walked quickly back towards the main building. She figured out which cabin was the caretakers' and silently sidestepped towards the tennis court. She knelt down once more and surveyed the crumbled surface. She looked around, headed into the lobby to retrieve her gear and went behind the desk to use the telephone.

She dialed zero. When the operator came on she said, "I need to make a person-to-person call from Doreen for Vincent Regazzini." She gave the operator the phone number and waited.

"Hullo?"

The operator said, "I have a person-to-person call from Doreen for Vincent Regazzini, will you accept the charges?"

"Yeah." Whoever answered sounded like he just woke up.

"Hey, Nick, it's Doe. Vinnie there?"

"Hang on." The phone receiver dropped. Doreen kept an eye out for Lorna.

Vinnie came on the line. "Doe! Whaddya know?"

"I think I found the location. It *is* that funky motel you thought it was. But I gotta hit the road. I'll call ya from Atlanta. I'm staying with Bambi for a few weeks." Bambi was Doreen's nickname for her mother. Her mother had large eyes and she always looked like she was staring into someone's headlights.

"Okay, good. Call me and we'll figure somethin' out. Say hello to your mother for me."

Doreen rang off and sat there for a moment. She felt a pang of loss. She actually liked Lorna. There was something real and sincere about her. Of all the women she had met in the last few months, Lorna was a cut above the rest. And boy, could she *kiss*. Doreen ran her fingertips over her slightly numb lips.

She closed her eyes and re-experienced the soft yet firm grip of Lorna's legs wrapped around her waist. It had turned her on quickly and she had had her own stealth orgasm from the pressure of Lorna's thrusts.

Doreen wanted a memento of their brief encounter. She eyed a beautiful pen, engraved with Lorna's full name and profession on it. Silver with gold swirl, and areas over the engravings worn to softness from years of use. She imagined Lorna's long fingers gripping the body of the pen, writing furiously and with purpose, doing her job. Doreen held it in her palm. She liked the heft of it. She would keep it safe and return it at some point in time—a good segue to come back to the motel even though she would have to explain why she took it in the first place—with the hopes that Lorna would not go *too* crazy trying to find it.

Lorna waded back towards the water's edge where she collapsed in the shallow water. With each sob, she felt her heartbeat sink down into a darkness of anguish she had felt only once before, and that was when Jeanie walked away from her, them, their magical, unconditional—or so she thought—love. Not even the death of her father evoked such fathomless murk.

Her body responded to the involuntary release of fluids and she wailed out towards the horizon, where if anyone could hear her, they would think an animal was in its final stages of death.

Where all this came from, how it untethered itself from her day-to-day composure, she did not know. She accepted the release and kept with it until she heard the sound of Doreen's motorcycle coming to life. The growl of the engine and the few short revs before the long drawl of departure made Lorna snap to attention. She croaked out, "God*damn* it!

No! Don't leave. Come back here and hold me. Give me your strength. Who *are* you?"

Reality took the place of emotional release now. Her current endeavor, her father's death, and break from her old life settled down around her like a soft blanket. A comforting cloak of warmth, which was the hot afternoon sun beating down on her bare shoulders, to assuage the raw exposed nerve endings. It was life, she reasoned, and in time, the changes *do* catch up.

She murmured to her fragile heart, "Sometimes it takes something like two good orgasms to unlock the hidden treasures. I read that somewhere in a book."

She looked up and down the empty stretch of beach. Miles of sand, shells, detritus from human kind scattered about. She then saw something floating lazily towards the beach on the incoming surf and realized it was her underwear.

She cackled in a thick, raw-throated way. Then started to laugh in earnest. "Only me."

She got up onto her knees and splashed the salty, healing ocean water on her face, through her hair, then tilted her head up to the sun. It caressed her face and she closed her swollen eyes, allowing Mother Nature to kiss her spent emotional reservoir.

She stood up, walked over to her twisted panties, wrung and shook it out, then trudged back to the log to retrieve her clothes. She got them on as best she could and headed slowly back towards the motel.

Tonight, she thought, she would invite Cheenah to join her in getting completely, totally, and unconditionally plastered.

ELEVEN
Saturday, June 21, 1980

Lorna was not quite sure how she got home but she remembers becoming very ill somewhere outside of an establishment. She recalls Cheenah having to call Anya to bring the van over to where ever they were. Lorna's car was a stick shift and Cheenah wasn't good at the "shift stick" thing. Lorna was glad she didn't remember too much about getting sick since she hated throwing up. But now, the morning after, she felt like absolute crap. The taste in her mouth was indescribable. Her eyes were very puffy, and her skin was mottled.

She knew she was most likely dehydrated, so she crept slowly down the stairs so the headache would not threaten to blind her and grabbed two containers of cold water from the fridge. She tried to drink slowly at the sink because she knew her stomach would not accept the cold liquid in fast order, but she was so thirsty she gulped the first few sips. Her stomach did a fast lurch for a moment then the nausea passed. She continued to sip the water and started to feel a little more human after finishing the first bottle.

She went back upstairs to survey the damage to her clothes. She couldn't find them. She was wearing a t-shirt and gym shorts and had no recollection whether *she* or someone *else* put them on her.

She stripped off her clothes and tossed them in the hamper. She turned the shower on and stepped in, letting the water pour down over her head and her body. She became lightheaded and held onto the shower caddy. When the dizziness passed, she put her head back and opened her mouth to rinse it out.

"God," she thought. *"What in the hell was I thinking?"*

Once dried and feeling a bit better, she drank the second bottle of water slowly. She sat on the end of her bed and looked at herself in the mirror. She was pale despite her solid tan. Her ears were ringing.

She thought she should talk to Anya and Milton. She walked gingerly next door to their cabin.

Anya came to the door. "Ay, you okay boss?"

"Barely. But better. Can you tell me what happened last night? I don't remember much."

Anya stepped out of the cabin. "Well, I think maybe you and Cheenah had a lot of fun. But then I think all the fun made you sick. Cheenah called us and I drove to pick you up at The Dockside. You were asleep on the grass when we arrived. Milton picked you up and put you in the van."

"Oh my God." Lorna ran a hand over her face.

"Oh, no problem, Miss. Everyone once in a while has to, how do you say, tie one on?"

"Yep, that's it." She belched silently. "What about Cheenah? Is she okay?"

"Oh, not to worry about Cheenah. She can drink anyone under the floor."

"It's *under the table*. So, she's not sick? No hangover?"

"Nope. No hungover."

"Wow. Good genes." She lowered her voice, "Hey, did you bring me upstairs?"

"Oh, *si*."

"And, my clothes?"

"Ah, yes, well, they were, uhm, stained a bit, so I took them to the laundry at The Palms."

"And my shoes?"

"Uhm, well, they didn't look so good, so Milton took them to hose them off. I don't think you will want to wear them again, Miss."

"Oh jeez." She groaned and shook her head. "I'm so sorry for all the bother."

"You must drink lots of water today, Miss. This I know from many binders."

"Benders."

"Oh *si*."

A few hours later, Cheenah brought Lorna's clothes back to her at The Pagoda.

Lorna sat in the cool lobby, nursing a glass of water with a cold pack to the back of her neck.

"Feeling better?" Cheenah put her hand on Lorna's shoulder.

"Oh my God. Like hammered shit. You've got to tell me what happened. Did I make a complete ass out of myself?"

Cheenah came and sat down opposite her on one of the chairs. "No, Miss. You behaved like a lady, for sure. You were just…very sad, is all."

"Sad?"

"You know."

"No, I don't know."

"About, well, Miss D…and all."

"Oh crap." She pulled the ice bag down over her face. "What did I tell you?"

"Uhm, most of things I think. How she made you cry."

Lorna sat quietly on the couch. She took the ice pack off and looked at Cheenah. "I can't be*lieve* you didn't get sick."

Cheenah shrugged. "Many years of practice, Miss."

"Are you telling me there is a lot about you I don't know?"

"Oh, *si*."

"Well, remind me the next time I call you to go out and tie one on that I should drink iced-tea and let *you* do the talking."

Cheenah smiled and said, "Our secrets, you and me, remember the partners in crime?"

"I do. Thank you, Cheenah. Sisters"

"I brought your clothes back. They are right here in this bag."

"I am so sorry you had to deal with that. Me getting sick and all."

"Is okay. You are better now, right?"

"Yes. Well, except for this ten-ton weight on my forehead. But yeah, I'm okay."

"So, what about Miss Doreen? Will she come back to here?"

Lorna found herself wondering the same thing. Somewhere in the back of her mind and heart she kind of hoped so. "I don't know. She's a bit of a drifter, so I'll say probably not."

Cheenah stood up and lightly rubbed Lorna's shoulders. "Okay, I will go back to The Palms now. You need anything, you call, *hokay?*."

Lorna took Cheenah's hand in her own. She said, "You're a special kind of friend, Cheenah. Thank you for coming into my life."

The next day, Lorna went to talk to Milton about her ideas for the Peace Garden. She was ready to get the job started, especially since the phone had not rung yet again for another day regarding the ad.

She and Milton walked back and forth over the surface. Lorna explained, "I would assume first we must dig up the asphalt. I would like to move the pagoda over here, make it a central focal point, know what I mean?"

Milton nodded. "I think so, a good idea. My cousin, he has an excavation business about an hour away. I will contact him. He is a good man. Fair. Not too much money to do the work."

"Why don't you call him and see if he is available to talk with me."

"It would be best if I talk with him. His English is not so very good."

"Sure, okay. See if he can come here maybe during the week?"

"I will call him *ahora*."

"Thank you, Milton. In the meantime, think about what plants might do well with the partial shade. And whatever kind of soil you will need. Just make a list of all the supplies and we can revisit it when I get a quote from your...what is his name?"

"Hernando, we call him Nando."

"Okay, when we hear from Nando then!"

"Okay, Miss Lorgana."

Lorna decided to call Steve.

"Hey Officer."

"Well, hi there! How are you?"

"Better."

"Were you sick?"

"No, just badly hungover. Cheenah and I went on a bender, or binder, as Anya calls it, on Friday night."

"Oh, boy." He chuckled.

"Hey, so, I was wondering about that golf outing. You still interested?"

"Oh, heck yeah! As a matter of fact, I was thinking of going over later after five. You want to join?"

"You betcha. I'll just get my clubs together and I can meet you?"

"How about I pick you up? And after we can go for a few drinks?"

"Uh, not me. I'll stick with iced tea."

"You got it. I'll pick you up at five thirty."

The rest of the day went smoothly for Lorna. She thought about Doreen only sixty times. She had such mixed emotions regarding what happened, but the truth of the matter was, setting aside the fact that Doreen seemed like a womanizer, Lorna was seriously attracted to her. There was something different about her. Maybe it was what she had to live with for most of her life. Maybe it was her family setting…a brother in jail, a mother who lived in Atlanta with some guy, her "uncles". It made sense to Lorna that Doreen wouldn't really want to set down roots anywhere, that maybe getting too close to people could be dangerous. But it didn't make what happened in the ocean the other day any less bittersweet. The fantasy evolved into a tug around her heart.

She hadn't met someone like that since Jeanie.

Golf with Steve was a lot of fun. It brought her back to the days when she went after a good challenge. Steve was an adept player. She even joked that her father, was he still alive, would admire Steve because he would give the man a run for his money.

"I used to find boyfriends that couldn't figure out which end of the tee to stick in the ground, and my father would get so *mad*!"

Steve laughed. "I'll bet your father was something else. So, you had boyfriends?"

"Yeah, but let's not ruin a good golf day. We can talk about that later, though. Yeah, dad *was* a tour de force. Someday I'll tell you all about him…and the boyfriends…*and* the girlfriends."

Steve said, "Well, how about tonight? I know a great place for grouper. It's kind of a dump but the food is second to none *and* they have excellent home-brewed iced tea."

Lorna nodded. "Just what the doctor ordered."

During dinner they talked about failed romances, one-nighters, Lorna's stand-in boyfriends to keep her parents at bay while she was in college.

"So, who taught you how to play golf?"

"My father. He had all of us on the links by the time we were ten years old. My brothers got to schlepp his clubs around and clean them before each shot, and I got to ride in the golf cart and keep score. He bought me a kids' bag of clubs and by the time I was thirteen, I was pretty proficient with them."

"Did you ever think of going pro? You remind me of Nancy Lopez."

"She's amazing. I'm flattered." She allowed the compliment to sink in. "I liked the game too much to make it a career. I had heard nightmares about quality of life."

"Well, there are some tough women contenders out there. Hey, maybe we should play with the sheriff. He and his wife play frequently, and truth be known, Marge is a better player than he is!"

"Let's!"

It was almost eleven by the time Steve dropped Lorna off.

Lorna was pleasantly pooped. Her hangover long gone, her spirit back to where it had been since she had moved south, her vision clear.

She was ready to start the next phase of the renovations. Thoughts of Doreen lingered on the periphery, but now that she had a new focus, she was glad to move forward.

TWELVE
Tuesday, June 24, 1980

When Anya and Milton came into the lobby on Tuesday morning to inform Lorna that Hernando was on his way over to the motel, they found Lorna on the floor underneath the front desk.

"Miss! What is wrong?" Anya knelt to be eye level with Lorna.

"I can't find my favorite pen! I *know* it was here on the desk before the weekend. But, for the life of me, I cannot find it! I've looked *everywhere*!"

The two of them scuttled around under the desk.

Anya said, "Well Miss, maybe a vacuum cleaning will help. It's a little dusty down here."

Lorna looked over at Anya. "Really?"

Milton leaned over, "You want I should look into the trash? Maybe it fell in there by accidental."

They heard the sound of two trucks entering the turn-around. Anya scooted out from underneath the desk. "This is Nando now. We can help look later?"

Lorna stood up, pulled her shorts out of her butt crack, and smoothed her blouse. "I just can't imagine where it is!" She didn't understand why Anya was giggling. "*What*?"

Anya pointed to her own rear end. "You got a panty problem? Maybe we have to excavate that too!" She let out a good laugh, her gold teeth gleaming in the ambient light.

Lorna raised her eyebrows. "Where do you come up with these things?"

Anya started to exit the lobby. "Oh, Miss…"

Lorna followed her wondering what was so funny about pulling her shorts out of her butt crack. She was surprised she did it in front of anyone. She usually reserved her bodily adjustments for the privacy of her own space. Must be that she felt like Anya was family.

Hernando Rubalcaba and his son, Gabriel, jumped down

from their large trucks.

Anya and Milton spoke to them in Spanish while translating for Lorna in English. The details seemed fairly straight-forward. When Nando surveyed the area to excavate, he took some measurements and used a small hammer-like tool to chip away at the surface. He didn't think it would take more than a day or two to break it all up. His son would drive the haul-away truck, and Nando would use the back-hoe.

After removing all the rusted hardware, Hernando and Gabriel began the process of stripping off the asphalt surface. It proved to be stingy. It was about a foot and a half deep. On day two, they uncovered the asphalt and found a solid layer of concrete stretching the length of the court.

There was a lot of banter back and forth between Hernando and Milton and Anya.

Milton tried to explain to Lorna, "'Nando says now that the top layer is off, maybe to stop digging."

"Why? Don't we want to pull all the cement out and refill with soil for the garden? Wouldn't we have to put a lot of soil to build up a base?"

"Well, yes, Miss. But he thinks the cement is very deep, maybe five or six feet, and his equipment is not strong enough to break through."

Anya added, "He says we will have to call other workers in with jack hammers to break up the cement. It could be very expensive, he thinks."

Lorna had to admit she was a bit out of her league when it came to these matters but she knew enough to know that cement was not a good base for a thriving garden. She asked Milton to ask Nando why he thought the cement base was so deep. "How could he know?" Anya translated.

There was a lot of Spanish going on and very little English in the translation.

Milton said, "Nando does not want to continue, Miss. He says he will break his equipment. He says it is okay to leave the cement base."

Lorna shook her head. "I disagree." She walked to the

edge of now broken up asphalt surface and stepped onto a patch of concrete. She turned to look back at the crew. "So, let's have Hernando and Gabriel clean this up and haul it away and call another company who can get through this cement."

Milton nodded and explained in Spanish. Hernando, with his hands on his hips, nodded and looked at Lorna. She got the distinct feeling that something was amiss. The hair on the back of her neck prickled a bit.

Hernando and Gabriel climbed back onto their equipment and began the process of clearing the rubble into the haul-away truck bed.

Lorna went into the lobby and called Steve. He might know of a company who did heavy labor.

"Sorry to bother you, but I was wondering if I could ask you a favor."

"Sure, what's up?"

"I started digging up the little court. Remember I wanted to make a garden out of it?"

"Yeah, I remember. A great idea."

"Well, we've run into a bit of a snag. Anya and Milton had one their cousins come by to strip off the top layer of asphalt and when they did that, they found solid cement underneath. They don't have the right equipment to break through it, so I was wondering if you knew of a company that might do that."

"We use a local outfit that works the municipal areas. Let me get the number here." Lorna heard shuffling sounds from Steve's end of the phone then he came back on. "Okay, Earl Driver and Sons. 466-9800. He's a good guy."

Lorna asked, "Do I need to get a permit for excavation?"

"Probably. Let me call you back in a few, see if I can expedite this for you."

Lorna rang off and sat at the desk drumming her fingers. She was very annoyed about losing her pen. She couldn't imagine where she had put it. Maybe when she was drunk the other night, she used it...for what? To write her last will and testament?

Lorna shook her head and started looking through the desk drawers one more time. Maybe it was buried underneath—

The phone rang. It was Steve.

"Okay, come on down to the station, and I'll take you over to the local office. The inspector has to come out and make sure there aren't any lines in the vicinity, things like that. In the meantime, give Earl a call and see if he can get you an estimate."

"Sounds good. Thanks, Steve. I'll be there in about a half an hour."

"See you then."

Lorna dialed Earl's number and spoke directly to him. He seemed like a friendly type, a little gruff around the edges. He told her he could come out later in the afternoon to see what she had going on.

Lorna went back outside where Anya and Milton were watching Hernando and Gabriel finish up their work.

Lorna said, "I've got to go to the Heatherton City Hall to get a permit to excavate. I called someone to come out later and give me an estimate."

Anya looked at Lorna. "Well, Milton thinks maybe you can put more top soil on the cement to make the garden."

Lorna looked at Milton, who looked away from her. "I'm a little confused. Milton, you're so knowledgeable about these things."

"Well, Miss. I…"

Anya interrupted, "You see, Milton is just trying to save you the headaches and money of more work that might not have to be done, *comprende*?"

"I understand but don't worry about the money. I want this done right."

"And the mess."

Lorna felt her temper rise a bit. "What is going on, you two?"

Milton offered in his quiet tones, "We don't know how deep, you see? It could be very deep."

"So?"

No one said anything. Lorna felt her hackles rise again. "What is *with* you two?"

Hernando approached them. He spoke to Milton. Milton said, "They are ready to leave. He says he will send you the bill."

"Okay." She turned to face Hernando, "*Gracias señor.*"

He nodded. "*D'nada. Adios, senorita.*"

Lorna went back into the lobby to collect her purse and keys. Anya and Milton went back to their cabin.

As she was leaving, she heard Anya and Milton using raised voices in their cabin. They rarely spoke to one another in angry tones, at least since they had been at the motel. What was going on? She started to walk towards their cabin but stopped midway. It wasn't her place to intrude.

When Lorna returned to the motel from filling out the paperwork downtown, she found Anya and Milton waiting for her in the lobby.

Lorna asked, "Are you two okay, you look troubled?"

Anya lifted her head and took in a deep breath. "We must go down to Boynton Beach. Our cousin Gloria has taken to be very ill."

Lorna frowned and looked at Milton. He averted his gaze.

"Okay." Her gut told her something wasn't quite right.

Anya continued, "Cheenah will go too. She and Gloria are very close, you see."

"Okay." Cheenah never mentioned a cousin named Gloria. "When will you be back?"

"Well, this will depend on whether Gloria passes on or not."

Lorna nodded her head. "Well, I'm sorry she is ill. You've never spoken of her."

"We have a very big family, as you know. You see, we were only told about Gloria just this morning. We had to talk to our cousins down in Boynton Beach to get the details and so on."

Lorna was not going to stop them from leaving but she had a very odd sensation flutter through her chest. Something was just off. "Will you call to update me? This is kind of sudden."

"Yes, we understand. We will call." Anya gave Milton a little shove and they left the lobby.

After they left, Lorna called over to The Palms. Cheenah did not answer the front desk phone. Her second-in-command, Paula McPherson, did.

"Hi Paula. This is Lorna over at The Pagoda. Is Cheenah available?"

"She just drove off the lot. Said she was going to be gone for a few days down south, a sick cousin. I had to rearrange my whole life to cover for her. Not that it's a bad thing, I could use the money, but still..." Paula, a heavy smoker, coughed away from the receiver. "Oh, this cough!"

Lorna thought, *"Maybe if you stopped smoking."* "Sure. Okay, thanks," she said.

When Lorna hung up the phone she definitely knew something was not right. It was *not* like Cheenah to *not* call her. Their friendship had blossomed to where they spoke every day.

This was very unusual.

By the end of the day, Lorna had met with Earl Driver. He surveyed the area and decided that a crew of five would get the job done in less time. His rates were reasonable. The process could start the following day pending the okay from the inspector.

This was the first time Lorna had truly been alone on the property since hiring Anya and Milton. It felt strange. She walked into each cabin, ran her hand over surfaces, surveyed the interior, breathed in the silence.

The whole place felt very peaceful, maybe too peaceful. She wanted to hear voices, see women come and go about their lives, reap the benefits of her hard work and good will.

She called Avril but got her answering machine instead. She left a quick message and rang off. She was still mystified about the disappearance of her pen. She sat at the desk tapping her foot.

No one was around. Maybe she would call Steve.

"Nah."

She decided to go to St. Augustine. It was a lovely evening. The sun was just starting to drop down out of the sky towards the horizon. The colors of the sunset were, as on par with northern Florida, simply lovely.

The motel was just too quiet.

THIRTEEN
Wednesday, June 25, 1980

The weather held during the morning of the excavation. There was a threat of a thunderstorm in the afternoon, but Earl and his crew were making good progress.

The sound of the hammers was deafening, so Lorna decided to head down to the beach.

As she was gathering her gear, Earl Driver entered the lobby. He didn't come all the way in because he was covered in cement dust.

He spoke quietly, but the tone of his voice gave Lorna a chill. "Uh, Miss Hughes, we have a problem."

FOURTEEN

Lorna followed Earl out towards the work area. It was quiet save for the hissing of the water in the hammer hoses. All the men leaned and stared down into the pit they had just unearthed. Lorna followed their gaze and saw what the problem was.

She had no words.

Earl cleared his throat and said quietly, "Ma'am, I think we need to call the police."

Lorna nodded numbly, lightheaded.

Earl asked, "Are you alright, Miss?"

"No. I think I might need to sit down." She turned away from the pit and walked unsteadily towards the main building. After ten steps she turned around and walked back to the pit, the possibility of what she *thought* she saw might not be the *truth*. She looked down into the pit again. Her head throbbed at the temples, the reality of what lay below her blurred her vision.

She mumbled, "*This*. Cannot be."

FIFTEEN

When she heard the sirens, she realized Earl Driver had gone to his CB in the truck to call the police.

Steve Kent pulled up first in a cloud of dust as he skidded to a stop in the turnaround. He got out of the cruiser, went directly to Lorna and looked down into the pit.

"Ah. Jesus," Steve muttered.

Steve continued to survey the pit while reaching up to his two-way located on a shoulder strap. "Marie?"

"Go Steve."

"I've got a 10-16 at the Pagoda Motel. You need to notify the local FBI office in Jacksonville. Keep it quiet, Marie."

"Ten four."

Another cruiser pulled up right behind Steve. The Chief of Police and another officer approached the scene.

Steve put his hand on Lorna's shoulder. "You okay?"

"Sure. Sure, I'm fine. Nothing out of the ordinary. Just a bunch of fucking human remains on my property. All in a day's work, right guys?"

She looked at the workmen. They avoided her glare. One of the men said, "Look, it *ain't* our fault. We was just doing a job is all."

A few of the other men chimed in. "Yeah, ain't our faults."

Steve said to Earl, "You and your crew need to stick around. I imagine the FBI will be here soon. Might as well have your men relax in the shade."

Earl shook his head, "Wait a minute, Officer. We got other jobs lined up for this afternoon."

Steve nodded. "I understand, Earl. But, unfortunately, this is now a crime scene."

Lorna turned away from Steve and Earl. The Chief approached Lorna.

"Miss Hughes? I'm Chief Sheriff Dan Goslin."

"Hello Chief," she managed to say. Her throat was parched.

He had kind eyes and was soft spoken. "This must come as a bit of a shock."

She nodded her head and snorted. "You *think*?"

He took her arm gently and guided her away from the scene. "Let's you and me go into the lobby and talk a bit, okay? Officer Kent has this under control." The sheriff nodded towards Steve and the other officer as if they could read his mind. They pulled yellow crime-scene tape from the trunk of Steve's cruiser.

She mumbled, "This *just can't be* happening."

SIXTEEN

"How about we have something to drink. Maybe some lemonade or iced tea?" Chief Goslin asked.

"I have a pitcher in the fridge, would you mind getting it? I have to make a phone call." She directed him to the kitchen.

"Sure. I can do that." He smiled at her and patted her arm as he passed her on his way.

Lorna picked up the phone and pressed the number two on her speed dial. When Avril answered, Lorna sat down heavily, put her head into her hand and quietly said, "I need you."

SEVENTEEN

Lorna waited for the sheriff to re-enter the lobby. She excused herself to go up to her bathroom.

The chief nodded and said, "I'll be down here when you're ready."

She closed the door quietly then sat down on the edge of the bathtub and put her head in her hands. She gasped and choked out a cry.

"Breathe," she muttered. "Just breathe. Avril will be here soon. We'll work this out. It's going to be okay. How in the *fuck* did this happen?"

A turn of bad luck.

But, why? Why now?

She splashed cold water on her face and towel dried it. In the mirror, her eyes were dark, and her mouth was set in a slim line. "Damn it," she said.

Lorna rejoined the sheriff when she composed herself. She was still shaky and bewildered.

"Better?" He smiled and handed her a tall glass of lemonade.

She took the glass and set it down on the table, "Yes, thank you." Her voice a monotone.

He waited until she sat down opposite him.

"Miss Hughes, do you know anything about the history of this motel?"

"No, actually, I don't."

He nodded and looked around the lobby. "You've done a good job fixing it up. Officer Kent keeps me apprised of the progress."

She wasn't in the mood for renovation chit-chat.

The sheriff cleared his throat and continued. "There is a bit of, well, shall we say *lore* about this property."

"Oh?"

"Nobody really knows for certain, but we believe that the motel was used as a safe house, a hideaway for the mafia back in the late '30s and '40s. What with it being so off the beaten track, know what I mean?"

Lorna nodded. "Go on."

"A Mexican family ran the place for many years."

"That's what Jim Tate told me. The Puentes."

"Good people, the Puentes, from what I understand. So, really, the discovery of these bones today probably gives more credibility to the mafia viewpoint. We think the Puentes were paid and paid well to run the place and keep quiet."

"So, you think those old bones in there might be some missing persons from the mafia?"

He shrugged, "Could be. I'm sure the forensics guys will get to work quickly. The FBI probably has a lot more intel, I imagine. We're just small-town cops here."

Lorna thought about it for a moment. While she was interested in the history, she was more concerned about what do to about it right *now*!

The rest of the day was a blur for Lorna. The FBI arrived, the lead agent named Carl Lawrence introduced himself to Lorna then started directing Earl Driver's men to hammer away at the swimming pool. Three flatbed trucks, a crane, and backhoe arrived all within the space of a couple of hours.

The FBI forensics team, dressed in white jumpsuits and sterile gloves and armed with small shovels, went down into the pit to extricate the bones. They worked slowly and with precision, setting the bones into lined boxes.

When the claw of the crane disappeared into the bottom of the pool, it brought up several rusted pieces of what might have been a vehicle. Various sized chunks of rusted steel, and a few flappy tires dropped out of the claw. They took several photographs.

One of the agents called out, "We got a plate, looks like Jersey."

Lorna was in full tilt panic mode as she watched her investment get pummeled with the hammers. She strode up to the group of FBI agents gathered around the pool findings.

She found the lead agent.

Her voice, pitched an octave higher than normal, came out rushed. "Agent Lawrence, are you planning on digging up the whole fucking place?"

He started to speak, and she cut him off, "Look, we *just renovated*! And I *just bought* the place! And and, I had *no idea* about *any of this!*" she shrieked.

"I understand, ma'am." He tried to calm her down. When he saw that she was on the edge, he called out to the workmen. "Take a break."

He said to Lorna, "How about we go into the lobby and talk for a while?"

Lorna scowled. "How about you take your men and machines and get off my property?" She knew she was being testy but couldn't help herself. She walked into the lobby with Steve and Chief Sheriff Goslin in tow. She did not offer refreshment.

She had to *think*!

The agent pulled a handkerchief out of his pocket and mopped his face as he made himself comfortable on one of the couches. "Air conditioning feels good."

Steve and the sheriff sat together on the opposite couch, and Lorna sat on the edge of one of the big chairs.

Agent Lawrence pulled a black notebook from his breast pocket and clicked a pen. "Can you tell me what you know of all this?"

"What I *know* of all this?" She raised her voice. "What I *know* of all this is just about what *you* know. Do you think if I had any inkling, I would have purchased the property?"

"No, I don't imagine you would have. Who did the inspection?"

"That would be Jim Tate. I have his card if you need to contact him."

"Yes, we will need to see his report. Did Mr. Tate indicate anything that might have given either him, or you, reason to question the *foundation* of the court or the pool?"

"No, he just said the condition of the pool and the court was such that repairs might be costly. I told him I wasn't interested in keeping either one for repairs and that the court would become a garden and the pool would eventually be filled in and repaved for a social area in the courtyard. He agreed with me and that was that."

"So, Mister Tate did not seem to think there would be a problem with excavating the areas?"

She sighed heavily. This was going nowhere. "He and I did not discuss it further. He thought my ideas of renovation were good. Increase the value of the property and so on."

Carl changed direction, "What was the asking price?"

Lorna fought the desire to tell him to shove his questions up his FBI ass. "It was low."

"How low?"

Lorna stood up. "This is ridiculous! What does the asking price have to do with—"

Carl made for her to sit down and remain calm. She tried to keep her anger in check. She said, "Look. Let's cut to the chase, okay? I had no idea about the history of this place before I purchased it. I've been on my own since I moved down here. Well actually," she added, "I have a live-in couple who caretake the property and the three us worked very hard to make it habitable."

"Who are the caretakers?"

"The Catalvos. Anya and Milton Catalvo."

"Do they live on the property? And if so, are they here now?"

"No, they are south, in Boynton Beach, visiting a sick cousin."

Just then something clicked in her mind. Something that had been nagging at her since Anya and Milton left so abruptly the other day.

"A sick cousin?" Agent Lawrence poised his pen over the notebook.

"Yes. A, uhm. a sick cousin." Her resolve quickly deflated, her body involuntarily sank back into the chair. Hearing herself tell Agent Lawrence that Anya and Milton were down south visiting a sick cousin became a crystal-clear reality, a clarity that brought her to a painful truth. Anya, Milton, *and* Cheenah…they all knew.

EIGHTEEN

When Lorna composed herself for the third time that day, it was agreed upon that the rest of the property would remain intact until further investigation could be made.

Agent Lawrence explained, "As you know, cold cases go on for years. We don't have a lot but what we *do* know is that the mafia had safe-houses all along the coast from Maine to Miami, dating back to, oh say, the early '30s. Keeping track of all the goings on was daunting, as you might well imagine."

Lorna nodded. "Go on, Agent Lawrence."

"Hall of records shows the building of the court and pool came long after the rest of the property was built."

Lorna said, "Okay, so the motel is built without a court or pool. Then many years later these two structures are added?"

"That is correct. The records—and they are a bit loose—show that the additions were made in the late 1950s."

Steve asked, "What about building permits?"

Agent Lawrence shook his head. "Building permits were bought and sold for a good price, especially the ones where the county turned a blind eye."

"Do you think the Puente family had anything to do with this?" Lorna asked.

Agent Lawrence answered, "Not really. Well, they may have *known* something about it, but I'm sure they were paid handsomely to keep it quiet. The actual owners of the motel *are* on record."

"Oh? And what was the name of the actual owners?"

Agent Lawrence snorted. "Smith. John and Dave Smith."

Steve, Lorna, and the sheriff all shook their head at the same time.

"A totally silent operation." Lorna thought about it for

another moment, "Makes perfect sense I suppose."

"It does," added Agent Lawrence. "Perfect sense and a

dead-end trail. Until now. I'm sure the forensics team will get the dating on those bones and they're probably twenty or thirty years old. It would certainly connect a lot of cold case dots."

"So where do we go from here, Agent Lawrence?"

"Well, I don't know what to tell you regarding future plans, Miss Hughes. But we should know in a few days if we have to dig any further. Until then, the property is still considered a crime scene."

Lorna nodded. *Great. Just fucking great,* she thought.

After speaking with Agent Lawrence, Lorna took a cool shower and tried to think things out. Her world was falling apart. This was such an unexpected chink in the chain. She toyed with the idea of putting the motel on the market after all was said and done.

Lorna towel dried herself and walked naked to her closet. She shook her head and chuckled despite the seriousness of the situation. A bitter mirth. It was all coming together. Anya and Milton's sudden departure, Doreen.

Doreen's father and grandfather were in the mafia.

Maybe she—the phone rang.

"Hello?"

"Hi, Lorna." It was Steve. "Have you had anything to eat lately?"

"Haven't had the stomach for it. But I suppose I should eat something. What did you have in mind?"

"The diner in town. Might do you some good to get away from the motel for a little while."

She agreed with him. She had to get away for a few hours. She was so overwhelmed.

In the car, she was quiet.

Steve drove his personal car instead of the cruiser and Lorna was glad for that. She couldn't imagine public knowledge of this ordeal yet.

He asked gently, "How are you holding up?"

"Not sure."

Steve waited until they were seated at the diner and the waitress took their order.

He said, "I tried to find more information in town regarding the permits for the pool and the badminton court. Nada. Zip."

"No big surprise there." Lorna moved the salt and pepper shakers around. "Steve, I have a theory. Work with me here." Lorna waited for Steve to nod. When he did, she continued. "Anya and Milton knew about this."

He cocked his head and raised his eyebrows. *"Really? How so?"*

"I didn't realize it until just a little while ago. First, a few days ago when their cousin Hernando arrived to dig up the first layer of the court, he stopped when he hit cement. He did not want to continue because he said that the cement would break his equipment and he didn't have anyone to jack hammer through it. Anya and Milton had to translate for me because Hernando did not speak much English. When there was a lot more chatter in *Spanish* than there was in *English*, I became suspicious. Like what they were talking about was something way more detailed than what they translated for me."

"Okay."

"And so, when I asked Milton about the base for the garden, he hemmed and hawed and couldn't look me in the eye. Anya stepped in, of course, and said Milton thought it would be okay to set the garden on the concrete as long as we put a good soil base underneath."

"Okay."

"Well, I thought about it. It would mean that the garden would be raised up off the ground several feet and unless I built a retaining wall around it with steps to get to it. It wouldn't work. I considered this for a while but didn't like the idea. So, I called someone at the garden Center and they confirmed that the best way to build something like this I should have at least four feet of earth to topsoil."

"Makes sense."

"So, I decided to dig up the cement, and that's when I called you and you gave me Earl's number."

"Right."

"So then, the next day, when Earl came by for an estimate, the Catalvos informed me that they were heading south to Boynton Beach to see a sick 'cousin'."

"Hmph." Steve nodded slowly.

"And Cheenah went as well. Drove her own car." Lorna added.

The food arrived. She continued explaining her theory while upending the ketchup bottle over her fries. "It came on so quick, so unlike them to not be more forthcoming. So, here we are, Steve. The Catalvos are MIA."

Steve dressed his burger. He seemed to be considering all the angles. "If the Catalvos knew about this and said nothing to you, it makes them…"

"Yeah." She waited a beat. "Complicit in a crime?"

He shrugged, "Not sure. Yet."

They ate in silence. Lorna realized she was famished as she polished off half her burger in three bites.

Two men walked into the diner and headed directly to the counter. One of them spoke to the waitress. "Hey Sal, did you hear the news?"

"What news?"

"That old Pagoda Motel up on Highway A1A, the one that just got bought by some lady from up north?"

"Yeah, what about it?"

"I heard that they just dug up a bunch of human bones."

She shook her head. "What the hell you talkin' about? And who is *they*?"

"I guess the owner wanted to make some renovations there, and when the guys dug it up, they found a shitload of human bones."

"Oh, come on, who did you hear this from?" She busied herself with filling the napkin holders on the counter. Other people started listening now. Lorna didn't move a muscle, and Steve put his burger down.

"Fred Lipton. He was one of the guys working for Driver."

The waitress guffawed and waved him off. "Lipton probably had too much whiskey before the job. The old drunk is a bit of a story-teller."

"No, the other guys confirmed it. And we just drove by there! The place is crawling with FBI. Big crane and trucks. What a mess. We tried to drive in but got chased away."

Sal considered this then said, "Well, holy shit. Whaddya know?"

Lorna stopped eating and started to get up. Steve held her by her arm and murmured, "Don't move." He got up and approached the men at the counter.

"Hey, guys."

They turned to look at him. "Oh, hey officer."

"Yeah, I need you to step outside with me for a moment."

They looked at him, "Why? Did we do something wrong, officer?"

"Please, just join me outside for a moment. Now."

Steve followed the men outside. Lorna watched them leave the restaurant. She could feel eyes on her back, as if all the customers knew who she was.

Lorna wanted to disappear. She pushed her plate back and folded her hands under her chin. Logic told her to sell the property immediately. Fill in the graves and sell it. Call it a bad move.

But she had fallen for her newly acquired Mexican family, and Steve—she just adored him—and everyone she met so far was so pleasant and easy-going. She had begun to carve out new directions for herself. She enjoyed the beautiful history of St. Augustine. She lived a new routine that suited her. And she loved the weather.

She didn't *want* to move!

But where *was* the family? Why did they abandon her? Her gut feeling of them *knowing* this was going to happen was not just a possibility, it was the *truth*. And she wanted to get to the bottom of it regardless of her choice to sell the property or not.

Steve came back in to the diner; the men did not.

Lorna did not want to know.

NINETEEN

Thursday, June 26, 1980
4534 Tropical Drive, Ocean Ridge, Florida

They spoke in Spanish.

Anya said to Marco's wife, Nancia, "You don't understand. Marco *must* come back with us."

Nancia replied, "It is so long since this happened, why must he go over it again and again? Can't you see he just wants to be left alone?"

Milton stepped in. "Marco, no one will hurt you now."

Marco paced back and forth in front of the big picture window that faced the ocean. "I cannot return."

Cheenah put her hand on Marco's shoulder. "Look Marco. All you would need to do is come back with us and talk to Miss Lorgana. She is very special, and we do love her very much. She is a good woman and she should have the whole story, the truth."

Anya said, "She will lose the motel. The police will close her down. And we worked so hard to make it look beautiful again. She has big plans. Please, Marco. Please reconsider."

Marco stopped pacing and regarded his family. They had grown up and played and went to school together.

Their parents were interchangeable. And while they all knew what had happened on that night so many years ago, they did not experience the steady stream of nightmares that he did.

They did not see what he saw. Marco slowly shook his head.

"I cannot."

TWENTY

Thursday, June 26, 1980
The Pagoda Motel

Avril managed to get on a morning flight. She arrived in Jacksonville at 12:30 p.m., rented a car at the airport, and sped down the highway to get to Lorna. She had no idea what to expect but knew that Lorna needed her.

When Avril pulled into the shambles of what was once the turn-around parking area of the motel, she slowly got out of the car and surveyed the wreckage.

Lorna ran out of the lobby and fell into Avril's arms. She shook with tears. Avril held her for several minutes, cooing soothing words, telling her everything was going to be okay.

When Lorna finally pulled herself together, she turned Avril away from the rubble and guided her towards the main building.

"How was your flight? Did you have any trouble finding the motel?"

"Well, that bridge you warned me about…wow, what a piece of shit! But no, it was pretty clear from your directions. I floored the rental, which I am glad to report did not fall apart, to get to you. I didn't really even look at the scenery."

Lorna nodded. "Let's get you settled, then I'll make us something to eat. I managed to get to the grocery store this morning but to be perfectly honest, I don't remember what I bought. I'm just so…"

"Sounds like a perfect idea! As long as you have wine, we are in good shape!"

Lorna smiled and nodded. "There's wine."

Avril sighed with delight when she saw the guest room. "It's absolutely *darling*! I just love it!"

She leaned on the windowsill and took in a deep breath. "Ahh. I've forgotten how deliciously salty the air is down here."

Avril decided to take a quick shower then unpack her suitcase. Lorna retreated to the kitchen to throw a simple meal of salad, tuna, and egg together for them. She bought some fresh-baked bread, sliced it, and set the small kitchen table with butter, jam, salad dressing, and utensils.

Once settled in with their wine and food, Avril regarded her friend. "So, I'll admit, you look, ah…tired. I'm so sorry all of this happened, Lorn. Things seemed to be going along so smoothly."

"The last few days have been such a tumble. But now that you're here I feel like I can breathe again."

Avril dug in. "Oh boy, this looks good. Didn't really eat on the plane. Okay, then. Tell me. Start from the beginning."

"The whole shebang?"

"The whole shebang."

TWENTY-ONE

Lorna and Avril went through two bottles of wine. After their meal they settled into the comfort of the lobby. By nine o'clock, they realized they were bushed.

Lorna was spent. She couldn't even talk anymore. They hugged each other and then parted company at the top of the stairs.

Lorna felt safe. Avril had such a calm way of parsing out the details then reassembling them for re-examination, which Lorna then took and built the rest of the structure with.

Together, they were going to take action!

Just what that would *be* had yet to be determined.

But she knew *one* thing for certain.

She was going to speak directly with Luis and Anita since they did not accompany Anya, Milton, and Cheenah down south.

Perhaps *they* had some answers.

TWENTY-TWO
Thursday, June 26, 1980

Lorna strode up the path to El Mocambo. The restaurant would not be open for business for another two hours. She found Luis and Anita at one of the tables going over receipts and paperwork.

She approached them. Anita said, "Oh Miss Lorgana!"

Lorna pulled a chair out from another table and turned it around to sit with Luis and Anita. She dispensed with the niceties and dove right in. "So, how is cousin Gloria?"

Anita cocked her head, "Cousin Gloria?" She looked at Luis and murmured, "Do we *have* a cousin Gloria?"

Luis looked at his wife for a moment then looked at Lorna. "She is…well, she is…"

"She is *nothing,* isn't that right, Luis?"

Anita sat up straight, the hand with the paperwork frozen in mid-air. "Now, wait just a *minuto*. What is this all about?"

Luis took in a deep breath. He puckered his lips and scratched his head.

Lorna couldn't help herself. "How come you didn't go down to Boynton Beach to be with Anya, Milton, and Cheenah?"

Anita was completely confused, "*Que,* Luis*?*"

Luis said, "Anita, please let me talk to Miss Lorgana alone, would you mind?"

Anita squinted her eyes, her lips in a tight downward curve. Luis kept his gaze steady on Anita's eyes. Anita screeched her chair back and harrumphed before storming off into the kitchen.

It was obvious to Lorna that Anita did not know much about this.

Luis tossed his pencil down and sat back in his chair. "Well, I suppose it was going to come to this eventually. What with you wanting to renovate."

"Start from the beginning, Luis. I don't have much by way of patience. And while we are at it, my name is *Lorna*, not *Lorgana*. I would appreciate you *all* learning that right from now *on!*"

Luis nodded. "I see that you are upset."

"I'm *damn* upset!" She pulled a newspaper from her purse and set it down in front of Luis. "Have you seen this yet?"

When Lorna had read the paper that morning, she almost blew a gasket. A reporter must have snuck in at some point in time to take a photograph of the excavated areas.

THE ST. AUGUSTINE DAILY JOURNAL
LET'S MAKE NO BONES ABOUT IT!

The sleepy little hamlet of Heatherton County isn't so sleepy this morning! An unusual discovery was made two days ago at the newly renovated Pagoda Motel. Owner Miss Lorna Hughes, Esq., formerly of Cleveland, Ohio, was shocked to find out that buried underneath her recently excavated badminton court were human remains.

Earl Driver of Earl Driver and Sons Excavation, Inc. was the first to see the find. He states that he and his crew were at the property to dig out an area for a garden.

"Well, when we first got there, the asphalt had been removed and we just started hammering down. The first chunk came out at about four feet. As soon as we were able to get the big equipment in there to yank it all up, we found the bones."

Miss Hughes was not available for comment. Local policeman, Steve Kent, said, "What has happened here is a shock to us all." Local FBI were reluctant to comment but did say that the remains were under investigation.

Also found underneath the swimming pool was an old rusted

van. It is purported that the van, with Jersey plates, was used to bring the bodies to their final resting place at The Pagoda Motel.

Further reports will be forthcoming. Pictured below:

The pit where the bodies were uncovered.

Luis read the short article then put the paper down. "What would you like me to do, Miss Lorna?"

"For starters, you can tell me what you know about this. I can't seem to get in touch with Anya or Milton or Cheenah. They just up and left. Left me in the lurch!"

Anita came back into the room with her own copy of the local newspaper. She regarded Lorna, a bewildered look on her face. She sat down heavily. "*Ay caramba*! What will be next?"

Luis sighed. "Let me go and lock the door. I think it is time we all talked."

TWENTY-THREE
Friday, June 27, 1980
Atlanta, Georgia

Constant ringing brought Doreen out of a sound sleep. Thankfully, her mother was awake and picked up the phone downstairs in the kitchen.

Doreen moved her long body around in the small bed. The guest room sported a twin. Her mother called up to her to grab the extension in the hallway.

"It's Vinnie. He says he has to talk to you."

Doreen grumbled. "Okay, I'll be right there."

She picked up the receiver and cleared her throat. "Vinnie, what's up?"

"You seen the newspapers?"

"What are you talking about? I just woke up."

"We were right! There was a small article in the *Miami Times* with a picture of that little crappy motel you stopped at up in St. Augustine. Seems as though the owner wanted to get rid of the tennis court and pool to make a nice garden. They found bones, Doe, bones!"

Doreen perked up immediately. "No shit! Well, go on!"

"Says here that the FBI's checkin' into all leads. Bone pieces will take time to investigate, all that bullshit that they do. And get this, they found a *van* buried underneath the pool! A friggin' *van*! Jersey plates! Gino was brilliant!"

Doreen nodded, a sour taste in her mouth. "Yeah. Brilliant."

Vinnie said, "You gonna go back there? I think you should. Y'know, put it all to rest."

"Yeah, probably." But Doreen's heart and mind spun, making her a bit dizzy. "Look, lemme get my coffee and wake up, Vin. I'll call you back when I decide what I want to do?"

"Sounds good, Doe."

Doreen went into the bathroom, shut the door, and sat

down heavily on the commode. She put her head in her hands and rubbed her eyes.

"*Damn* it."

TWENTY-FOUR

Doreen knew from a very young age that her life was different from most of her school chums. While the DiLaRusso's lived in a special kind of 'community', Doreen went to New York City public schools. Most of the kids were cool, but there was a group of girls, the boys were too afraid of their fathers, who made fun of her family mob status.

"Does your father steal money from poor people?"
"Who did *your* daddy kill today?"
"Is it true you buy things with dirty money?"
"My mother says your father is a *stoonade*!"
"Your brother is greasy."
"Do you eat pasta every night? Is that why you're fat?"

Doreen *was* a very chubby little girl. She ate to pad to her fragile soul. It did not matter how much her father instilled a tough-guy attitude so she could defend herself, she always thought of herself as less-than.

When Doreen was fifteen years old and had braved the worst years of junior high school, she started to tone her body, get serious about being tough, and finally open both eyes to the reality of her familial upbringing.

She also watched her father take two bullets, one to his head and the other to his heart.

It was a Friday night at Geracci's Pizza Parlor in Queens. The Steggliano Brothers owned several pizza joints around the Queens and Bronx areas and Friday nights usually boasted a big crowd since tap beers were half-price.

On this Friday night, a designated family night for the DiLaRusso's, the restaurant was unusually quiet. One of the Stegg brothers was in the kitchen throwing dough and the other one was out on an errand.

Doreen's father seemed a little uneasy as he filled his ample belly with fresh pepperoni pizza. Doreen's mother thought it was nice that the restaurant was quiet.

"I like being able to hear you guys talk without feeling like I need hearin' aids!" She commented.

Then three men walked in.

There was an audible slap as the pizza dough landed on the floor from the open kitchen.

One of the men reached inside his inner coat pocket. The other two men moved to flank the gunman.

Bobby DiLaRusso stopped eating. He put his pizza slice down, looked at his family, then said, "I love you. All. Very much."

Doreen's mother stood up, the gun man told her to sit down and to not move.

She started to scream but the gunman pointed his pistol at her face. The few other patrons slid under their table, hoping to avoid crossfire.

Bobby turned to shelter his family.

He said, "Not in here. Outside."

The gunman nodded. Bobby stood up. Doreen froze, her panic rising.

"Daddy! Wait!" She squeaked.

Bobby faced his daughter, a little piece of pepperoni stuck to the corner of his mouth and leaned down towards her. "You. You're the strong one in the family. You take care of your mother. Your brother, he's not so smart. You're the one who has to carry on, my sweet baby girl. You'll go down to live with Vinnie in Florida. You'll be safe there."

Doreen stood up but the gunman motioned his pistol for her to sit back down. "Daddy. No! Don't go with them." She started to cry.

"I have to baby girl. I have to pay for what your grandfather did a long time ago."

Bobby walked out of the restaurant with the gunman behind him and the other two goons following.

He did not turn back. When they walked around to the side of the restaurant, Doreen bolted from her chair, knocking it over, and ran out the door. She turned the corner in time to witness the gunman, at close range, put two bullets into her father's body.

Bobby DiLaRusso slid down the brick wall. He turned to

face his daughter. He located the stuck piece of pepperoni on his mouth, licked at it, smiled, tried to wink at her, then dropped like a sack of flour, the alleyway brick grit covering the back of his green golf shirt.

Doreen ran. She ran and ran and ran.

She'd been running ever since.

TWENTY-FIVE

Friday, June 27, 1980

At the same time Anya and Milton were driving back north to Heatherton County, Doreen was loading the last of her gear onto the Harley. She was going to head south, back to The Pagoda Motel.

Cheenah remained in Ocean Ridge to try to convince Marco to come with her. She offered to pay for a return plane ticket from Jacksonville back to Palm Beach when all was said and done. His resolve slowly dismantled. He knew how important this was to Cheenah, Anya, and Milton. And maybe if he shared what he saw, the ghosts would eventually just fade away.

Cheenah sat with Nancia in the the Puente's kitchen. Marco was still asleep.

"You know, he always liked you the best." Nancia took a sip of her coffee. "He said you were different, but like, the same as he."

"Yes, I liked him, too. Since he was the only child, what was not to like?"

Nancia chuckled. "He doesn't talk much about it, you know. He sometimes has nightmares. He wakes up in sweat and with screams."

"Don't you think it is now the time to rid himself of these night dreams?"

"You know, we've had many good times, but he's not all himself. I wish so much for him to enjoy life totally, you know what I mean?"

"Of course."

"And it is very generous of you to pay for his plane ticket back home."

"It is what you do for family, no?"

"Oh, *si*."

They sipped their coffee in silence, both women looking down at their half-empty cups. Cheenah asked, "Do you regret not having children?"

Nancia looked up. "Oh, Cheenah. I wanted to have babies. But Marco refused. He went for the surgery very young, you know. He said he was too afraid of leaving his baby without a father. And me, he was so very protective. After we returned from Mexico, he said he would work very hard to give us a nice home, but we were not going to have babies."

They were silent again.

Nancia took in a deep breath then stood up. "Well then, I must go wake Marco and pack for him his bag. He *will* go with you today."

Cheenah smiled. "I think you are making the right choice, Nan. The past must go away now, and soon, you and Marco will come to visit at The Palms. Like old times, maybe?"

"Like old times. Maybe...even better!"

They hugged and Nancia headed down the hall towards their bedroom.

Cheenah waited until she heard the bedroom door close then went immediately to the phone in the hall. When she was connected to her party, she said, "He is coming with me. We will leave soon. We will be there later. We will go straight to Miss Lorgana."

Luis said, "I'm glad you convinced him. Anya said he was too scared to come. Oh, and Cheenah, you must call Miss Lorgana Miss *Lorna* from now on. She is very mad."

"I can understand this. Have you heard from Anya and Milton?"

"Just a few minutes ago! They will be here this afternoon. We decided that we must go together to see Miss Lorna. They will come here to the restaurant first and I will tell them you are on your way with Marco. Maybe they will go to The Palms to rest after their trip. Why don't you come straight here, then we will all go to see Miss Lorna."

Cheenah heard Marco and Nancia speaking to one another in the other room. "I must go now. We will see you later, Luis."

"Drive safely, my sister."

She went into the guest room to repack her suitcase, then take a shower.

It was going to be a long day.

TWENTY-SIX
Saturday, June 28, 1980
The Pagoda Motel

Lorna's heart skipped a beat when the phone rang.

"Hello?"

"Hello Miss Lorna, this is Luis."

She was expecting his call. "Are they all there?"

"*Si*, Cheenah just arrived with Marco. They are just freshening up at The Palms."

"Well, bring everyone here. It's time to get this all out in the open."

"Yes Miss, it is."

Lorna hung up and looked at Avril. "Show time."

Avril patted the couch next to her, "Come sit for three minutes, will you? You're wearing me out."

Lorna obeyed but sat on the edge of the couch, bouncing her leg. "I feel like a caged lion."

"I know."

"My motel is in shambles."

"I know."

"I'm so pissed off. I feel so *betrayed*."

"I know."

Before Lorna could say anything else, she heard the growl of the engine. She listened for a moment as the growl came closer to the motel. She stood up and went to the door. Avril followed.

"Oh, for Christ sake...," Lorna mumbled.

Avril watched as Doreen maneuvered the Harley around the rubble in the turn-around. "Well, well, well. I take it that's the famous lover?"

Lorna nodded then went out the door.

Doreen shut down the bike. The hot pipes ticked in the late afternoon heat.

Lorna approached her. "This is not a good time, Doreen."

Doreen started to take off her helmet. "I have to talk to

you."

"This time you should have called."

"Lorna, we have to talk."

Lorna looked at her. She was, despite the fact that she had most likely been traveling for hours, still absolutely stunning. Lorna's body and mind battled once again. She fought down the desire to pull her into her arms. "Might this be about the recent news of..." she nodded her head towards the large opening in the ground.

Doreen said, "Yes, it is."

Lorna crossed her arms in front of her chest, her voice clipped. "I'm not sure how I feel about you showing up right now but you might as well stay. It's all going to go down, anyway."

"Whaddya mean?"

Lorna started to walk back towards the lobby, "Just wait out here, okay?"

Doreen nodded, hung her helmet on the handlebar, and walked to the edge of pit.

Lorna entered the lobby.

Avril said, "Humpty Dumpty has *nothin'* on you right now."

Lorna leaned on the front counter, her head in her hands. She said, "You know, I played out how I would react if Doreen ever came back. I wavered between running back into her arms and telling her to fuck off."

Avril came up behind Lorna, wrapped her arms around her shoulders, and laid her head on her back. "Oh honey. Your poor heart. Why don't you send her away?"

"Because I think her arrival today is serendipitous. She might be the mafia key."

Avril thought about it for a moment, "You might be right at that."

Ten minutes later, the caravan arrived. First Anya's van, then Cheenah's tan Chevy. They all disembarked from their vehicles and walked around the yellow-taped pits.

Anya and Cheenah looked at Doreen. Doreen watched

them watch her. Anya scowled. Cheenah narrowed her eyebrows and pursed her lips. Doreen stepped around them carefully.

Lorna went out to the turn-around. When she saw Anya, Milton, and Cheenah her emotions splayed like a jellyfish preparing for flight. She wanted to yell, cry, shake them, hug them. She said nothing but watched as they walked gingerly around the taped excavated graves. They looked small, defeated. Even Anya's defiance seemed to deflate.

Luis approached Lorna with a man by his side. "Miss Lorna, this is Marco Puente."

Lorna reached out her hand. The poor man looked like a scarecrow. "Hello Marco, I am Lorna Hughes. Luis has told me a lot about you."

He nodded and took her hand. His grasp was soft, his eyes watery. He bowed his head. "Thank you, Miss, for seeing me today."

Lorna's resolved softened momentarily. "You are welcome, Marco. Thank you for coming."

Anya approached Lorna.

Lorna crossed her arms in front of her chest again, prepared for battle.

Anya said, "Miss Lorna. I think maybe it would be best if we could all come in and go right to the kitchen."

Lorna was pleased that Anya finally got the memo about calling her by her given name. "Why the kitchen?"

"The painting on the wall. I told Marco you did not cover it up. He says it will help him to explain things."

"Okay. Let's get going."

Anya assembled the troops and they went single file, heads bowed and silent, into the main building.

Lorna looked at Cheenah as she passed by. Not a single phone call while she was away. Nothing to connect them. So much for the *sisterhood*.

Doreen was the last one to enter. Lorna looked her square in the eye. Blue met green with a jolt of lightening between them. All Lorna could do was breathe in the essence of Doreen. She smelled like wind and engine. Lost was the bravado.

Lorna said, "You look tired."

Doreen nodded. "You don't even know."

Once assembled in the kitchen, Lorna and Avril went to the front of the pack.

Lorna put her hand on Avril's shoulder. "I would like to introduce you to Avril Klane. She is my dearest friend and was kind enough to come to my rescue when the rest of you decided to run."

Anya, Milton, and Cheenah exchanged looks with each other and put their heads down.

"So, who will start?"

Marco cleared his throat then raised his hand. "I will speak." Cheenah gently took him by the elbow and brought him in front of the mural, near the sink.

Marco looked up at the painting. All eyes were on him. He crooked his head this way and that and a slow smile came over his face. "Such a *bonito* day this was, remember everyone?" He turned to face his family. They spoke in low tones.

"Of course."

"I will never forget."

"Look how happy we were."

"I miss them, our parents."

"We shared everything."

Marco continued to speak, his voice so soft, almost a whisper. "You see, Miss, I was only seven years old here at this time. This is my mother, Tita, and this is my father, Diego." He pointed to two of the four adults in the painting. He was portrayed running towards them with laughter on his chubby, happy, childhood face. His mother had her arms open to him and his father was smiling down.

He continued, "This right here," he leaned over the sink and tapped his finger on a little girl. "This is Alianah." He turned to face Anya.

She whispered, "Yes, that is me."

Lorna wanted to ask her why she never shared that the

people in the mural were her family, but she turned back to Marco, who moved a bit down the counter and said, "Ah, this is Cheenah and Luis. They were always getting into mischief those two." Cheenah and Luis were near a tree and had their heads together in some sort of plan.

"I see now," Lorna nodded.

"And these people here, are Consuela and Cesare. They are the parents of Anya, Cheenah, and Luis. Consuela and Tita were sisters, but not blood sisters. The Puente family adopted Consuela."

"Who painted the mural, Marco?"

"*Madre*."

"Very talented. She really captured the moment. Tender and loving."

Marco turned to face Lorna. He clasped his hands in front of him at his waist. "I loved my family so very much. It was so hard, that day, when I had to leave. When I told them about what I saw, they were so very afraid for my life. I remember papa and uncle Cesare sitting me down and explaining how important it was that I did not say anything to anyone else." Marco sighed deeply.

Lorna approached him and put her hand on his arm. "Do you want to sit down, Marco?"

"No, no. I am fine right here." He looked to Cheenah who nodded her head for him to continue.

"Miss. You see, when I was to become eighteen years old, my family gave to me a very wonderful party. It was at The Palms where Cesare and Consuela were caretakers. I had my very first girlfriend then and we planned, for so many weeks, to meet that night of the party back here," he raised his hand toward the ceiling, "so we could be…together." He cleared his throat then continued. "So, I hid my bicycle in the bushes at The Palms, then rode very fast to come back to get things ready, you know, make sure everything was just right. We planned it, you see, to wait until everyone had much to drink and would not miss us."

Lorna nodded. She could picture the night clearly. An eighteen-year old boy nervous and excited about becoming a man.

"When I came back here to The Pagoda, I saw Mister G with all these men in white shirts with the sleeves rolled up to the elbow. There was a big tractor with a big claw on the front and a cement mix truck. They must have worked quickly because the equipment was not there when we left for the party just a few hours before." He started to pace. "You see, there were two big holes in the ground already and then, there was this other truck, a van, with the doors come up right to the very edge of what turned out to be the tennis court hole. When Mister G and his men opened the doors to the back of the van, they yelled for the people inside to get out. You see, their hands, they were tied behind their back, like this." Marco demonstrated then continued, his hands slightly shaking. "Then the men and Mister G lined these other men up around the edge of the hole, you see. Then Mister G took a shotgun and started to kill the men standing at the edge of the hole one by one with *rapido* fire. A few of these men tried to run away but they got shot in the back. Mister G, he ordered his men to pull the other bodies back and then throw them into the hole with the other bodies."

Complete silence in the room.

Marco looked over to Cheenah who nodded her head for him to continue. He said, "I had to wait for Marianna, so I stayed behind the bushes. I did not want my beloved to see what was going on. I could barely keep my breath. When I saw her coming towards me on her bicycle, I quickly met her and told her we had to return to The Palms. She did not know what was going on, but she saw how scared I was.

"When we arrived, I told her I had to speak with my uncle, Cesare. I told her to go get him and bring him outside. I did not want to go back into the party. Because if I told my father, he would go immediately to The Pagoda, and I did not want him to get killed!"

Marco took a deep breath to steady himself, then continued. "So, I told uncle Cesare what I saw, and at first he did not believe me. But he must have believed me soon because I started to…crying very hard. He told me I had to tell my father *right away*. He tried to calm me down and told me when *he* was younger, he saw lawmen kill two very famous criminals in a cottage near to where he worked to pick oranges with his father, and that he hated violence."

Lorna wondered why Cesare ever came here in the first place if he knew that the mob owned the very motels they worked in, got paid for, raised their kids in. If he knew that violence was a big part of the job description of being in the mob, why subject his family to it? Unless, of course, he really did *not* know what they did.

"You see, miss, it was almost two o'clock in the morning, and Cesare and Diego snuck over to The Pagoda. They watched as the cement truck filled in the big holes. The very next day Mister G presented to my father a new little court and swimming pool. It was so very hard to be as we were and not let on that we knew what he did. If he found out, it would mean we would lose everything or maybe end up in some hole in the ground, too. It was then a rule in our families that *no* one, no matter *what,* was to speak of what was buried under the grounds."

Avril took in a deep breath and murmured, "Good God."

Marco continued, "My family was very worried that Mister G would find out I knew, and so then I had to go live with my father's brother, Bernardo, in Mexico City. At least for a while."

Lorna gently asked, "Marco, who was Mister G?"

A choked voice came from the back of the group. "Gino DiLaRusso."

All heads turned towards Doreen.

Marco looked directly at Doreen. "You know of this man?"

Doreen stepped to the front of the group. "Yes. He was my grandfather."

Marco visibly paled. He stepped back from her and then blurted out in one breathless sentence, "Please, please, I did not do anything for so many years I told only my family and my family sent me away to keep me safe because they thought Mister G would kill me if he found out I knew about the bodies." He crumpled against the counter and put his head in his hands. "So many bodies." He shook with sobs.

Cheenah went to him and put her arms around his shoulders. "Is hokay, Marco. Come on, is hokay, you are safe here." She scowled at Doreen who had her face in her hands.

Marco spoke under his breath in Spanish.

Lorna went to him and held his hand. "It was very brave of you to come here today. Cheenah is correct, you are *safe*, Marco. The past is gone now."

TWENTY-SEVEN

Lorna moved the group out of the kitchen into the lobby and waited until everyone was comfortable.

"First of all, I want to thank you for coming back. I don't have to tell you it's been a very rough couple of days." She paused here then stated, "I am seriously considering reselling the motel."

This elicited gasps.

"When I bought this property, my wish was to provide a place where creative people could *create*. Where the atmosphere would be kind, gentle, and rewarding. Are you following me?"

They all nodded.

"Things were going along so well. Anya, Milton, Cheenah, you three were my world. You kept me focused, you kept up with your tasks, showed me that this could be done. You accepted me and my sexuality so… quickly. I truly thought I was building a new family, one that cared, and shared a vision of sorts. We took this beat-up property and made it habitable again."

Nods and murmurs.

"Oh yes. We worked hard."

"Yes, it has come so far."

"Yes, it is so beautiful."

"Then a stranger arrives on the scene." She looked at Doreen. Doreen tried to smile but instead pinched her lips together and nodded slightly.

"She arrives at my doorstep, seemingly interested in my ad for renters, but now I see that she is back here because there *is* history here for her. Did she know that when she arrived on our doorstep that day a few weeks ago? Yeah, I think she did. Did she realize that the motel where her grandfather committed his heinous crimes was one and the same offered in *The Connection* ad, and that she had hit paydirt? Yeah, I'm pretty sure she did. So, was I surprised when she just happened to return here to the motel, *today* of all days? Not really. Fate was working its charms."

Doreen bowed her head, her hands clasped between her knees.

"But I digress. We are here today to figure out why after so many years, the remains of brutal murders are finally unearthed. Why didn't any of you say anything? Do you all realize you might be complicit in a felony?"

This was not true, but she thought a little sensationalism was called for.

There were more audible gasps.

"If I had not thought to dig up the court to build a garden for my tenants, none of this would be happening. But I *did*. And I should have followed my gut when *you* guys," she nodded towards Anya and Milton and Cheenah, "took off down south for a *fake* sick cousin."

Anya interrupted quietly and said, "But Miss, we *do* have a cousin named Gloria, only she lives in California. And she is *well*, however—"

"Anya!" Lorna pursed her lips and continued. "I should have stopped you and demanded an explanation! My God, you guys, why didn't you talk to me? Was I that unapproachable?"

The sound of the overhead ceiling fan provided some white noise while everyone waited. Lorna crossed her arms in front of her chest and paced. "I will stay here all night until one of you has a believable answer."

Milton stood up. "Miss Lorna. It is because we love you that we came back as quickly as we could. It was our reason to leave. We had to go to Marco to convince him to come back with us. At first, he refused. But after Anya and I left him, Cheenah was able to persuade him to come with her. He was frightened of coming back here, but you see, he has been living with his frights for many years now. Back then, there was no going to the *policia*. There was *no one* to tell because everyone in town was, how do you say, paid away to keep quiet."

Lorna nodded. She understood how the mob worked from reading and watching movies. But, *hearing* about it first-hand made it more plausible that Marco had to carry this horrible secret around with him for his entire adult life, with *only* his family to protect him, and for them to keep quiet as well for their own protection.

Luis said, "You see, Miss Lorna, the Mexican family is very strong together. We protect our own. When Marco had to leave us, he went with other relatives who he could not tell. Maybe our parents did the wrong thing by sending him away, but they were so very frightened for his life. And he was so scared. He was not well from then on, Miss Lorna. He just gave up on life. And we missed him so very much. Diego and Tita, they could not have any more children for some reason, and Marco was all they had. They had *us,* but it wasn't the same."

Lorna asked, "Did Mister G ever find out? I mean, if Mister G did not know Marco witnessed the murders, why would Marco have to leave his family?"

No one spoke for a moment.

Then Anya stood up and Milton sat down. "Because that is how we did things, Miss Lorna. We were all very scared at the time. All we knew is that we were well cared for."

Lorna said quietly, "Yeah, well cared for to keep quiet for *them.*" She looked over at Doreen who averted her eyes back down towards the floor.

Anya pleaded. "Miss Lorna. I must ask of you *not* to sell the motel. It is so beautiful. You made a great movement—er, uhm—*move* from Clevahland. Milton and I and everyone made things beautiful again for your guests. We saw how much you wanted these things to work. We were just scared, is all, and we did not know how to make it right. We thought maybe if we went down to bring Marco back it would make things right again. And maybe he could be right again, too."

"I appreciate that, Anya, I really do. But I must understand why you didn't tell me about things when I started to dig up. I put a lot of trust into you three. We could have worked this problem *together*. It didn't have to go this far."

Anya sat back down.

Cheenah stood. "Miss Lorna. We did not know *what* to do. When Miss Doreen arrived unexpectedly and said her father had been killed in the mafia, we were very worried that maybe she was sent by Mister G's family to...uhm. Well, to take care of..."

Lorna guffawed. "Cheenah! I can't even believe I'm hearing this!"

When no one said anything, Lorna realized with stark-raving clarity that maybe they did think the story wasn't over yet...that revenge could come at any time. But revenge for *what?* These people were no more involved in the crimes committed so many years ago than the man in the moon.

Lorna shook her head then looked at Doreen. "Care to comment?"

Doreen looked up from staring at her clasped hands. Her face pained. "I think I can clear a few things up." Everyone turned to face her. "Do I have to stand?"

Lorna, despite her mixed feelings about Doreen at the present time, had to stifle a chuckle. "No. You just have to talk. The truth."

"I've been thinking a lot about this on my trip down here. I haven't slept much so, I hope I can make sense." She cleared her throat and stretched her neck and shoulders. "Lorna, I apologize for coming here under the disguise of being interested in your ad. Well, actually, I thought the concept was, *is* pretty fantastic but...I was after something else."

Lorna leaned against the stereo cabinet. She watched Doreen's mouth move, her beautifully shaped mouth.

"See, in the *family*, there is a pecking order. Like, one guy is the top man and then everyone underneath him is more like a...a...I dunno, like a service man. There's a whole lotta levels, see. My grandfather was the top man for many years. He had so many different levels under him that I don't even understand all of it. He ran all the deals, assigned his crews, opened clubs and bars, ran gambling joints from one end of

New York to Miami. He was highly respected. He was known throughout the family as the brains behind all the operations. You didn't mess with Gino's operations. If you did, well, then…" she paused, "so, from what my uncle Vinnie tells me, Gino found out about a group of guys who were running a scam in the family. They were double-dipping into some big funds. They thought they could get away with it, but they never made it. It was the dumbest thing to try to outsmart Gino. His connections ran so deep. So, Vinnie tells me that when Gino got wind of it, he rounded up the bad eggs and brought them here. The motel was clearly out of the way and no one would be the wiser. See, those guys—the ones who tried to get away with stealing from within the family— are the ones who were buried underneath your court, Lorna."

"Jesus…" Lorna and Avril exchanged glances.

"In the family, all things come around. Know what I mean? Even the top man isn't safe. Even though Gino kept his security guys around him at all times, they couldn't keep an eye on *everything*. There is always some kind of revenge going on within the family. It's such a complicated mess, really. You guys still following me?"

Everyone nodded.

"So, one night while Gino was playing the horses at Saratoga and eating at his regular table in the clubhouse, someone poisoned his food and he died later that night."

The Mexican crew gasped.

"There had been a vendetta out for not only him, but his first born who was my father. It wasn't enough that Gino bit the dust. My father was next in line to pay for it."

Doreen cleared her throat and continued. "See, I was there the night my father was gunned down. I too, have nightmares that never go away." She looked at Marco.

Marco nodded in kind.

Doreen said, "I will never forget what my father told me right before it happened. We were all having dinner at our regular pizza joint on a Friday night. The goons came in the door and my father, like, he *knew* it was finally his time. He made them take him outside, but before he went out the door, he leaned down to me and told me I was to take over the business because we all knew that my brother wasn't big in the brains department. Dad whispered in my ear that he loved me the most. I watched him walk out the door."

She swallowed. "Then I ran outside in time to see the goons plug him with two bullets. One to his head, one to his heart. In the *family*, it was known that the last bullet goes into the heart. So, the victim doesn't forget, even in death."

Lorna felt her resolve soften. She couldn't imagine watching her father getting gunned down. She had no words.

Doreen continued. "My family was quickly relocated to Miami to live with Vinnie and his boys. My father's wishes were that Vinnie should take care of us and teach *me* everything I needed to know about running a business. I *never* wanted the responsibility. I thought the whole mob thing was awful. I just wanted to learn about engines and cars and how to fix things. I didn't care about anything else. My life had changed so much." Again, she looked over to Marco.

Lorna asked, "So, who ran the motels when Gino died?"

"His next in line. A real scumbag named Vito Carnatelli."

"What year was this?"

"Oh, let's see. I was seven years old when Gino died, then fifteen when my father died. I'm twenty-eight now, so…nineteen fifty-nine? Yeah, that sounds about right."

"So, what made you want to find out what happened here?"

"Curiosity, mostly. Vinnie was trying to educate me on the family and who was who. All I knew was that Gino was very powerful. A powerful *madman*, I thought. I also wanted to know why my father had to go. It wasn't fair. But, nothing in the mob was fair. I guess I wanted to put the past behind me, y' know, just clear it all away once and for good. I had heard the stories about Gino, but I needed to know for sure. So, when I first came here, I was certain this was the place."

Lorna thought about something for a moment then switched gears. She looked directly at Anya. "Anya, who owned the motel before I came along?"

Anya sat up a little straighter in her seat. She looked at Cheenah and Luis, who shrugged their shoulders and nodded in unison.

Milton whispered, "It's okay, Anya. Tell her."

"Me."

TWENTY-EIGHT

Lorna did not see this coming, but it was all starting to make sense to her. She thought back quickly of all the times Anya just seemed to know where to go for repairs on the property.

She encouraged Anya to explain.

"You see, Miss. Diego and Tita went back to Mexico in the early part of nineteen and seventy. It was decided that Cheenah was to run The Palms because *our* parents wanted to go back to Mexico to be with Diego and Tita. I would take over at The Pagoda. Well, it was good for maybe ten years. Milton and I kept things up and we had many *touristas* in and out, some always came back."

"But then something very awful happened in Mexico, just a few years ago. Did you hear about the hurricane named Idris?"

Lorna nodded, it was devastating, one of the worst storms in history. It took out a good portion of the northern Gulf coast of eastern Mexico.

"Diego, Tita, and our mother and father died. The storm, it washed away most of the town they lived in. It was very bad. We had lost our parents. It was a very, very bad time."

There was a heaviness in the room. Cheenah reached for a tissue from the box on the end table, Luis and Anya grabbed each other's hand.

"It is still so very hard to this day to know that our parents died in that way."

Lorna shook her head slowly. Her resolve gone.

Anya composed herself and continued. "So, you see Miss Lorna, when this horrible thing happened, we all went down to Mexico with the money our parents had left for us and helped to rebuild the town. Also, Milton made the designs for a very big garden in honor of our parents in the center of the town. It is very beautiful. It is called the Alvarez-Puente Arbor."

"Anya. I don't even know what to say." Lorna felt her heart become heavy. "I didn't know. I am so very sorry about your parents. Your loss." She looked towards Marco and Luis. "I am just, so very sorry for all of you."

Anya continued, "So, when we arrived back here, Milton and I put the motel for sale. Unfortunately, it had gone downhill while we were away. Anita stayed back here to run the restaurant, and Cheenah came back and forth because she had to take care of The Palms. You see, Miss, we just wanted to be done with all of it."

Lorna completely understood. Everything made perfect sense.

"We stayed with Luis and Anita and then after some months we took the job with Mister Johnston. I came to the motel once a week while it was on *for sale* just make sure things did not get too bad. We had the new windows installed, did some minor plumbing work."

Lorna now understood now Jim Tate's comment about solid foundation.

Silence. The overhead fan, a gentle breeze coming in through the windows, the clearing of a throat, a small cough, and sigh or two gave Lorna the time to collect herself. It was, in a sense, over.

The truths were out and on the table.

Lorna asked quietly, "Is there anything else anyone would like to say?"

When no one spoke up and everyone looked bedraggled and worn out, Lorna said, "Thank you, all of you, for clearing the air. I know that *I* am completely overwhelmed and exhausted and I imagine you all are too. Why don't we stop here and get some food, sleep, and maybe tomorrow morning things will look very different."

Anya agreed, "Yes, Miss. I think that would be good. Milton and I will go now to our cabin."

Cheenah stood up. "Come Marco, you will stay with me."

"Yes, I must get back to the restaurant and Anita." Luis stretched his long limbs, his joints audibly cracking.

Avril had gone into the kitchen, leaving Lorna and Doreen alone in the lobby.

The look on Doreen's face was one of defeat and sadness.

Lorna fought the urge to approach her, hold her. Instead she said, "I am so very sorry about your father, Doreen. I can't even imagine."

Doreen nodded her head. "Yeah."

Lorna approached her. "Will you stay?"

"Where, here?"

"Well, maybe at The Palms?"

"Lorna, I don't belong here."

"But, you're tired. You've been traveling a long time. You shouldn't get back on the road tonight."

"I'm used to it."

Lorna felt her heart continue to soften. "Maybe... you might think about changing that?"

Doreen sighed then chuckled, "Honey, I've been on the road so long...it's the only thing that keeps me moving forward. I haven't stayed in one place long enough to get a change of address, know what I mean?"

Lorna moved closer to her. "Why don't you just stay the night? Get some food, rest. Maybe you and I can talk tomorrow?"

"Well, I suppose I could do that."

"Promise me you won't take off in the middle of the night or something?"

"That's a bit odd for you to say that. After all, wasn't it you who sent me away in the first place?"

"That was different. I'd like the opportunity to explain some things."

Doreen regarded Lorna. "Okay, maybe we can do that. I'd like that, actually."

"Will you call here tomorrow after you've rested some?"

"I will. Can you write down the number for me?"

Lorna went to the desk and grabbed a piece of paper. Doreen approached the desk and gently laid the pen down on the counter top. "You might need this."

Lorna looked at the pen then at Doreen. "You...my pen! How did you...what the...?"

"I nabbed it when I was here two weeks ago."

Lorna shook her head and snorted. "You have this way of catching me at every turn. Why would you take my *pen*?"

"Because it's you. It's beautiful, all worn and soft on the barrel there. I wanted something to remember you by."

Lorna had no words.

Doreen continued, "Look, I know it was stupid, childish even. But something happened that day in the water there. Something that I'd been careful to not let happen in my life. Kissing you, holding you, feeling you against me. It felt so...right."

Lorna came around the desk. Doreen stepped back as if Lorna was going to strike her or something. "Okay it was just a pen. No need to—"

Lorna stood very close to Doreen, their breath intermingling.

"Oh, just shut up, will you?"

Lorna leaned in, took Doreen's face gently in her hands and kissed her gently on the cheek. She stepped back and said, "Go get some rest. Don't you dare leave in the middle of the night."

Doreen reddened slightly but visibly relieved. She said, "I won't. Now that everything is out in the open and I've returned your pen, I guess we can start over, right?"

Lorna chuckled lightly. "In *this* place? One never knows where something is going to go."

TWENTY-NINE

Avril came out to the lobby only to hear the engine of the Harley recede. She had two wine glasses. "I've got some soup on the stove. You must be famished. I take it Doreen is riding off into the sunset?"

"No, she promised me she would stay the night at The Palms. I called Cheenah and reserved a room for her." Lorna reached for the wine. "I feel like I've just been on an LSD trip."

"Hah, who are you kidding? You've never done LSD!" She sipped her wine then asked seriously, "Have you?"

Lorna shook her head, "No." She sighed and stretched her body this way and that. "This whole thing is so surreal, though."

They both plopped down on opposite couches. Avril said, "What a story. My God. Meanwhile, in other news around the country…"

"Yeah."

Lorna sipped her wine, "Oh, that's good. I can feel it searing down through my bones. I've been such a wreck."

"Well, at least this whole thing is out in the open. And you can move on. You still on the fence about selling the property?"

"Oh, Avril, a good night's sleep might sway me one way or the other. You know, while I was so busy being pissed off at the *betrayal*, it seems as though the very betrayers did everything they could to keep it together in the throes of a twisted past. I have to respect them for that."

Avril nodded. "True."

"And I don't think Doreen and I are done yet."

Avril raised her eyebrows. "Uhm, hm. I saw the sparks between you two. She *is* pretty attractive. But her personality. She seems to have so much baggage."

"Don't we all?" Lorna regarded her friend. "I mean, none

of us bring *just* a backpack through life, right? Sure, her life was, maybe still is, in turmoil. But she didn't sign up for it, she was born into it."

"True. But why should you have to walk her through it?"

"I don't know. Sometimes I believe that helping others through things can help the helper to heal."

"Unless the person you're helping takes advantage of that."

"It's a risk."

"Are you willing to take that risk after all that has happened here?"

"I think so. Who knows though…it's her journey. It wouldn't be that hard to let her go at this point. It's our chemistry that seems to click right now."

Avril said, "But I don't want to see you get hurt."

Lorna shrugged. "Well if I do, I do. If I went through life in protection mode all the time, I wouldn't live. I *was* living that life in Cleveland. And it was killing me. Sure, it's been a crazy ride here, but…I'm living!"

"So, you think Doreen might stick around?"

"I hope so. She has nothing to lose but time. And time seems to escape her."

"So, you'll take it slow with her?"

Lorna nodded, "Oh yeah. Painfully."

"And what about the Mexican crew?"

Lorna set her wine glass down. "That's part two of the story and I'm not ready to dissect *that* yet. At least not until I've had a good meal and a good nights' sleep."

Avril tossed back the rest of her wine. "Good because I'm starving and that can of soup on the stove looks pretty dismal."

Lorna stood up. "I'm taking you to the Crab Shack. The food is unbelievable! It's a little humble dump right on the pier. You'll *love* it."

"And you *know* how I love humble dumps."

They left the lobby without cleaning things up and drove over the intracoastal towards St. Augustine. Lorna felt her strength of conviction return. She probably would not sell the property. Now that everything was unearthed, she could start fresh. And the media stir was quick, thanks to Steve for keeping things down to a mild roar.

"Maybe," she reasoned with Avril as the evening air permeated the car, "the whole reason that the phone didn't ring after placing the ad was because somewhere in the universe a sign was beaming out that The Pagoda Motel was *not* ready for business. Not just yet."

Avril nodded, "Uhm hmm. You might be right at that."

They drove in silence over the intracoastal.

Lorna thought, *a few more repairs are still needed. And then it will be ready for new life.*

THIRTY
Three Months Later
September 1980

Doreen parked the bike in the lot. The dunes of Heatherton County were just a couple hundred feet away. They took off their riding boots and walked towards the surf barefoot.

"This is such a beautiful spot, Lorn."

"I love it at sunset. The colors, the clouds. Might see some cloud to cloud lightening."

They sat down in the sand close to each other, their legs touching at the knees. Doreen breathed in. "You ready for Thursday?"

"I'm very excited. You and Milton and the crew did an amazing job. The succulents are already growing faster than I can keep up with. I love the smell of the garden at night. It's so peaceful, Doe."

Doreen nodded. "It is a work of art, I'd say!"

Lorna looked at Doreen. "So are you."

Doreen leaned in to kiss her. "Flattery…"

Lorna settled her head on Doreen's shoulder after they kissed. Doreen sifted sand through her hand. "So, what's my next project, boss?"

Lorna wasn't sure how to answer this question. She wanted Doreen to stay on. They were starting a very comfortable—hot—romance, but Lorna also knew that Doreen wasn't one to stay somewhere very long. Lorna tried to keep her feelings in check, doling out just what she felt safe with, but at times she could not hold her heart back, especially during their lovemaking. She was falling for Doreen.

Doreen broke the silence. "No jobs on the docket?"

Lorna turned to look at her. "Will there always have to be a job?"

"What's that?"

"Will there always have to be a job to keep you

interested, here, with me, us?"

Doreen continued to sift sand through her hand. "Are you worried I'm going to get bored and leave?"

"Yeah, of course I am."

Doreen nodded and said nothing.

Lorna learned that Doreen kept her feelings close to the vest, allowing just a certain amount out at a time.

During a phone conversation with Avril one night when Doreen left to go back to The Palms where she was staying, Avril pointed out a hard truth to Lorna.

"You know, as far as longevity goes, Lorn, you haven't had the staying power, either."

"I know."

"Ever since Jeanie, you've bounced around from person to person. And I'm not that I'm saying that to be cruel."

"I know. I get it, Av. I'm just as new to this as she is. Only, she can get on her Harley and zip away. Never to be heard from again. I stay in one place and wallow."

"Do you guys talk about this at all?"

"I'm a little nervous to bring it up, I don't want to seem clingy. We are enjoying each other's company right now. She's working her butt off on the renovations. She and Milton are as thick as thieves. They are a lot alike in that they like the quiet, they don't talk a whole lot, and they work hard."

"Interesting."

"She tolerates Anya. Anya thinks she is keeping her in line for me. Cheenah flirts with her to no avail. It's working out pretty well, I'd say!"

Avril laughed, "So, where do you think this is going to go?"

"I want her to stay. I've offered her a cabin. She's thinking about it."

"You think that's a good idea?"

"Well, she can't stay at The Palms much longer. She's paying a low room fee but she's starting to feel closed in. I thought maybe if she had her own space, she would feel better about sticking around, and plus the fact, she spends most of her time with me at the motel. She maintains everyone's vehicles. She's even joked around about building me my own Harley."

Avril laughed. "Hah! You would be so hot on one of those!"

"I love the way it feels. She's teaching me to drive hers, but I know she gets all nervous if I can't keep it steady. It's pretty heavy."

"It's her baby. I could understand that."

Doreen interrupted Lorna's thoughts. She asked, "You gettin' hungry? You want to hit the Crab Shack?"

Lorna blurted out, "I want you to stay here because you want to. Not because you have a job to do."

Doreen said nothing.

Lorna asked, "What do you need from me, to make you stay?"

Doreen pivoted in the sand and faced Lorna. She put her hands on either side of Lorna's face. "I've got what I need, right here in the palms of my hands."

"But what if it's not enough?"

"I could ask you the same question, you know. I could never measure up to Jeanie. Not in a million years."

Lorna pulled away from Doreen. "I hate when you compare yourself to her. Do you know how many people I've alienated in my past because I thought they never measured up to her? I'm so mad I allowed myself to do that. And I vowed I would *not* do that again."

Doreen pulled her back closer again. "For as much as you're scared that I'm going to split some night, I'm just as scared that you'll think if I'm not working on something, or being *useful*, I won't make the grade."

"Oh my God…do you really feel that way?"

"Yeah, I do. I've been worried about it since we're done now with the renovations and all."

Lorna lightly traced the scar on Doreen's face, ending at her chin. "I don't think you have anything to worry about."

But Lorna was cautious. Scared that she would open her heart fully and lose it in the matter of a single, pivotal

moment.
   Like the moment in 1964.

Cleveland Ohio, 1964

Lorna walked up the path to the front door. It was a beautiful warm Spring day. She knocked on the latched screen door.

Jeanie's mom came to the door. Instead of letting Lorna in like she usually did, she stood behind it talking to her through the dark weave.

"Oh, hi Lorna."

"Hi, Mrs. Doyle." Lorna tried to look around Mrs. Doyle towards the steps that went up to Jeanie's little 'apartment' on the top level of their house.

"Well, Jeanie is entertaining right now."

Lorna said, "Oh!" Lorna figured one of their posse was upstairs with her.

"Yes, Aaron is here."

Aaron Silver. A gifted musician with a brilliant future to Juilliard School of Music. He was a nice enough guy, but Lorna knew he was attracted to Jeanie in a big way. Jeanie liked him because he was so talented and nice. Because he was a guy. Because Jeanie was scared of being labeled a lesbian. Because she didn't want to lead the lesbian lifestyle.

At all.

Lorna felt her heart seize.

"You can call her later, he's staying for dinner."

Lorna nodded but couldn't move. She knew exactly what was going on in that upstairs apartment. The classical music, the incense, the bean-bag chairs on the floor, the sunlight streaming into the room, warming everything around them, dust motes dancing in time with their breath. Aaron's head in Jeanie's lap while Jeanie stroked his face. Or visa-versa.

Done. Gone.

Over.

Just like that.

When Lorna finally found her legs, she turned and walked away from the screen door, down the path towards the sidewalk, towards her bicycle, towards a world that just became fractured. Her instantaneous pain became heavy and dark. So heavy and dark that nothing in her right mind could hope to fix.

***

Lorna turned to Doreen. "Maybe someday you'll tell me about why you feel safer on the road, jogging from location to location."

Doreen shrugged. "No ties."

Lorna said, "No home. Well, kind of. I guess. Maybe wherever you hang your helmet is your home until you feel like you need to keep moving?"

Doreen dug into the sand with her toes, staring out into the vast Atlantic. "It's not easy, you know."

"What isn't easy?"

"Running."

Lorna looked at Doreen. She did not want to disturb the moment by asking questions. She turned her head back to the ocean and waited.

"You know, after I saw my father get shot, my world went black." She dug a little deeper into the sand, so her toes were covered. "His face, as he was sliding down the filthy brick wall in the alleyway there, it was almost as if…he winked at me while he was licking a piece of pepperoni off of the corner of his mouth." She chuckled with a grimace. "He fucking *winked* at me while going for the fucking pepperoni."

Lorna held her breath.

"He was my dad. The tough guy. Plugged with two bullets in the family fashion. And he was trying to get that last…little piece…of fucking…pepperoni."

Lorna let her breath out slowly, waiting.

"I couldn't decide if I should laugh or cry or scream or…"

Lorna watched from the corner of her eye as Doreen had covered her feet now up to her ankles in sand.

"So, I ran. I ran home. I could hear my mother screaming

my name, I could hear my brother's footsteps comin' after me. All I wanted to do was close my eyes against the vision I had just witnessed."

Lorna fought the impulse to put her hand on Doreen's shoulder.

"The funeral. The people. The house, all the commotion. I felt so lost, like I was floatin' in jello or somethin'. That Monday my mom pulled me out of school. Most of the family helped us pack up the house. The next thing I knew we were on a plane to Florida, never to return to New York again. My whole life shifted. Every time I heard a car backfire, I thought it was gunshots. I couldn't watch violent movies, or even be in the same room with the television goin' during a crime show. It made me sick to my stomach. I was so nauseas all the time. I could barely eat. I was so…lost, Lorna. I vowed that I would never get close to anyone. And if I did, I would purposely fuck it up so bad that the other person would ditch me because they didn't know what to do with me. I hurt a lot of innocent hearts, Lorna. I have a pretty scary reputation." She took a breather.

Lorna waited.

Doreen continued. "So, when we got settled in Florida, I buried myself in the garage business with my cousins, learned everything I could about engines, carbs, trans. I didn't have any friends of my own…just stayed with my cousins, went to school because I had to. Just kept my eyes focused on the road and as soon as I got my inheritance, I was fuckin' gone."

Lorna sighed. "Oh babe…"

Doreen mumbled, "I wouldn't blame you one bit if you told me to leave again, and this time for good. I'm a fuck-up, Lorn. Never went to college. And here you are a lawyer. You're smart. Me? I just know about fixing things and using my hands. I feel so broken." She hung her head. "Aw God." She squeezed her eyes shut and shook quietly. She murmured between tears, "Aw God…"

Lorna finally reached over and put her arm around Doreen's shoulders, pulling her close. Lorna could feel deep wracks work their way up through Doreen's chest and out in the form of very sad moans. She remembered a day not too long ago when she bellowed out towards the big ocean and felt her insides crawl up through her throat, the pain burning her lungs as she wept.

Lorna whispered, "You're not broken, baby. Maybe just a little...torqued."

Doreen managed a chuckle. "Good way to put it." She sniffed.

Lorna said, "You don't have to run anymore honey. Just be who you are, give your heart a rest."

Doreen turned and fell into Lorna's body, sobbing openly.

Lorna wrapped both her arms around Doreen's shoulders and rocked her gently in the sand.

The moon was the only illumination in the room.

They spoke in low tones, soft and gentle. Lorna lay with her head on Doreen's chest, Doreen's arms holding her close. Lorna stroked the soft skin around Doreen's upper thighs. She ran her hands slowly up and around to the upper part of her pubic hairline, tracing a path to her navel and up over her tight abs, using her palms slowly to massage out towards her sides and ribs.

"Thank you for trusting me enough to share your pain." Lorna said quietly.

Doreen ran her hands through Lorna's thick hair. "You're different, Lorna. I knew that from the first moment I laid eyes on you. I felt a connection right away, but of course, had to deny it."

"Yes, I understand that," Lorna sighed. "You know, I pretty much did the same thing you did. Every relationship I had after Jeanie was more like a conquest."

Doreen asked, "How do you mean?"

"Well, of course, I compared everyone to Jeanie. And then when no one measured up, I started thinking that no one would be able to open my heart like she did. What I realized, though it wasn't *her* that I couldn't find. It was me. I refused to open my heart, thinking that no one really deserved it. That no one could spark the magic."

"So, you just compared everyone, but really, it was you?"

"Pretty much."

"Sounds like maybe no one had a chance, then, right?"

"Bingo."

Doreen shifted her weigh so she could see Lorna. "So, you're kinda like me in that you're scared, right?"

Lorna nodded. "Yes. On so many different levels. Heartache and pain all the way around when you think about it." She leaned up on her elbows and said, "Do you ever feel like if you could take your heart out of your chest and let it rest for a while—but still be able to breathe and live—and purge all the bad stuff out before putting it back into your chest, it would feel like a clean slate?"

Doreen chuckled, "Well, now. There's an interesting idea, Lorn. Kind of like...take it out, rinse it off, maybe use a little hydrogen peroxide?"

Lorna giggled, "Oh, my God! That would feel so *good*, donchu think?"

Doreen added, "Yeah, then maybe a little WD-40 to get the creaky parts back in working order."

They started to cackle, saying ridiculous hilarious non-sequiturs, eventually detouring a perfectly soft and gentle evening of lovemaking with an all-out pillow fight.

Out of breath and sweaty, Lorna—on her knees with a pillow clasped in her hands—said, "If you decide to ditch me in the middle of the night, I will come looking for you and not stop until I find you. And if you fuck it up purposely, you will live to regret it. You got that, DiLaRusso?"

Doreen, on her knees as well with a pillow clutched in her hands, replied, "If I do anything that stupid, I would expect you to come find me. Maybe even a public spanking would be in order."

Lorna tossed the pillow aside and moved her body flush with Doreen's. "You would be the biggest dumbass if you left me to keep running."

Doreen's lips grazed Lorna's, "You got that right."

Their lovemaking was heated and emotional.

Lorna felt every lock around her heart burst open.

This was it.

Doreen whispered, "Here we go, Lorna Hughes. You think you're ready for this?"

"I am…so ready. Are you?"

"It's outta my hands now, babe."

Lorna slid herself on top of Doreen and traced Doreen's face with her mouth. "You always smell like the outdoors, like the wind. And right now, like me." She kissed her forehead, nose, and traveled slowly around to her temples, cheeks, and ears. Before landing on Doreen's lips, she looked into her eyes. In the dark, the blue looked lighter in color, almost iridescent.

The connection between them strengthened without words. Lorna felt Doreen's arms tighten around her. She had never felt so secure as she did in this moment.

Not even with Jeanie.

THIRTY-ONE
Friday, September 16, 1980
The Pagoda Motel

With a clear sky, the temperature moderately warm but not suffocating, the air not as humid as it was in the summer, Lorna stood up to address the attendees.

She looked behind her at the newly renovated garden, the water feature provided a sweet gentle rushing sound. Her heart was full-to-overflow. Her family—Avril and Saul, Anya and Milton, Cheenah, Marco and Nancia, Anita and Luis, Steve and his new girlfriend Jillian, and Doreen—sat in folding chairs waiting for her to speak.

"I don't even know where to begin. The last six months have been…" she felt herself tear up. They waited for her to compose herself. "Have been life altering. When I made the decision to embark on this journey, I never thought it would pan out the way it did. Maybe I had unrealistic dreams of everything falling into place at once, like a story book or something. I never anticipated the history of the motel. But, that's life, don't you think? Cheenah, you were my first real friend here. And from there on, you all became my extended family. You accepted me into your lives right away. I never questioned your trust for one moment. Not even when you knew the whole thing was going to be exposed. You went to Marco to convince him to come back here to close the gaps. It showed such loyalty."

"Milton," she looked at him and smiled. "You are so talented. Your eye, but more importantly, your heart. You are a kind, gentle man, and your dedication to Anya and her family is so simple and true." He responded by nodding his head ever so slightly and smiling.

Lorna shifted her gaze. "Anya. I could not have done this without you. Steve Kent said you were the boss and he was right. In the aftermath of your parent's untimely death, you continued their legacy of love, of life, and of heart. Granted, you can be a little hot-headed at times, but I have come to depend upon you more than you'll ever know. Your dedication to the renewal of the motel, and to me, will never waver from this point forward."

Anya lowered her head and said quietly, "This is all very true, Miss Lorna."

"And Cheenah. You *are* my sister in crime! You have given me a sincerity that I've not experienced before. You've taught me so much. I only hope I can return the strength and friendship you offer with as much love."

Cheenah said, "You do."

"Luis and Anita. Your food, your dedication to the community, your acceptance of me. Wow."

Anita smiled and put her right hand to her chest, the left wiped a tear from her eye. She murmured, "I usually cry at the weddings, but this…well.."

"Marco and Nancia. I hope you will come often to see us, the past is behind you and will never again cause you fear. You are just as much a fixture here as the rest of your family. You are always welcome at The Pagoda. Thank you for coming up today for this dedication."

"Steve. I feel safe knowing you are on the job. But above and beyond, you are a great friend. Like a brother. You kept me safe during the excavation mess, kept the talk in town down as much as possible. How can I repay you?"

He chuckled, "Have a bad day on the golf course and let me win once in a while!"

Lorna winked at him and smiled, "Hah! Fat chance."

Lorna turned towards Avril and Saul. She felt herself tear up again.

"Avril. The sister I never had. You are my life connector. You are the linchpin that keeps me on task. You have been there for *every* up and down. Your sense of humor, the way you lay everything out and put it all back together again to make sense again, it's uncanny."

Avril interrupted, "It's from having children."

Lorna smiled, "Ah, you had that talent long before the

kiddos came along."

Saul nodded. "One of the reasons I married her. She keeps me in line."

Avril playfully slapped Saul on the shoulder then kissed him on the cheek.

Lorna continued. "Av, I know you tried to get me to rethink this move to Florida, and for a split second there I almost did. But I didn't, and you followed me here in spirit. You've always been on the other end of the phone day or night and when the shit hit the fan, you were on the next flight down. I am honored to be your friend."

Avril wiped a tear from her eye. "Oh great! You *would* have to make me cry."

She turned. "Doreen."

Doreen flushed and tried to maintain her cool. "Uhm, ahh."

Lorna laughed. "For such a tough guy you can be awfully gentle and sweet. Your past, your history. You brought it here to get closure. The timing was as it was supposed to be, don't you think? That first day you arrived on the Harley. You turned my life on its heel."

Doreen took in a deep breath and said, "You weren't the only one, for sure. That's why I took your pen."

Anya sat up straight and looked at Doreen then to Lorna. She said, "Aha! So *that* was the big mysterious of the lost pen! Remember Miss, the day you could not find your favorite pen?"

Lorna chuckled. "I do."

Anya looked at Doreen and pointed her finger at her. Then she started to laugh. Doreen started to laugh, then everyone—including Lorna—started to giggle out loud.

Lorna waited for everyone to settle back down. "So, without going on and on, I want to unveil the plaque today." She went up to the rebuilt pagoda in the center of the garden and pulled a piece of fabric off a black framed sign that she would have Milton plant after the dedication.

"To Anya, Luis, Cheenah, and Marco. May the memories of your beloved parents always stay in your heart. May your hearts stay open to the new memories yet to be made. Lorna Hughes, The Pagoda Motel, September 1980."

Lorna could not hold back the tears this time. "I love you all. Thank you for coming into my life."

THIRTY-TWO

After the dedication party—which lasted all weekend—and after things got back to routine, Lorna had a professional photographer come to the motel to take pictures of the newly renovated public areas.

She called *The Lesbian Connection* and took out a half-page ad. She had the pictures situated in between the copy. She wanted the phone to ring.

And ring it did.

Lorna, Anya, and Doreen took shifts to answer the phone. In the space of two weeks, Lorna had a file folder crammed with possible renters.

Since she only had four cabins available—Doreen took the one-bedroom cabin across from Anya and Milton's cabin—Lorna had to be selective in her choices. So far, from the fifty or so calls she received, she was interested in six of them.

Over dinner in the main building, Lorna discussed some of her choices with Doreen.

"So, here's one from New York City. Her name is Paris Katherine Todd. She calls herself P.K."

Doreen said, "Ooh, I like the name."

"Yeah, it caught my eye. She's a singer songwriter. She performs in clubs around the city, and she's looking to write material for her first album. She plays guitar."

"Hmm, sounds like it might be nice to have some music on board, don't you think?"

"Yeah, I think so! I liked the way she expressed herself. She sounded…grounded. Like, she knows what she wants, she sees her future in the music business."

"Sounds solid."

"She said it would be the perfect opportunity for her to write. Quiet, peaceful. She said she's getting claustrophobic in the city. Wants to spread her wings. Wants to expand her creative reach. She's tired of writing about urban grit."

"I can understand wanting to get out of the city, for sure. You can't spread your wings very far, know what I mean?"

"Do I ever." She sorted through another folder. "Okay, here's one. Sam Harper. She's a writer who wants to publish a book on, of all things, the lesbian life! She said she was going to send me some samples of her work. She said the ad excited her because she was looking for an environment where lesbian women shared their lives. Who knows? Maybe she could write about us!"

Doreen stood up from the table, taking dishes to the sink. "What a gas, huh? I can see it now. She writes about the life here at the motel and what everyone does and all their business and whatnot. A real Pagodaville!"

"Pagodaville." Lorna drummed her fingertips on the table. "I like it. I like it a lot. You know, if you think about it, we're already there. What with all of us kooks running around here."

"Hey, speak for yourself!"

Lorna guffawed, "You're the biggest one of all!"

Doreen turned to face her while dripping soap and water off a dish into the sink. "What? Your nutty tribe started long before I got here!"

"True. But all the new additions have added a whole other dimension."

Doreen came back to the table, leaned over and kissed Lorna on the head, then looked down at the file folders on the table. "So, who else you got lined up?"

"Let's see." Lorna shuffled some papers. "Lindy Sutton, a graphic designer, from Atlanta. She looks good. Here's one I thought was kind of interesting. Alice Puntston. She calls herself 'Lucky'."

"Hmmm." Doreen returned to the sink and turned on the spigot. She added, quietly, "Wonder if she bets on the horses."

Lorna turned to look at Doreen, who had her back to her. She said, "Old habits die hard, eh? You like to go to the races?"

"Well, I don't have box seat like Gino did, but I like to watch 'em run. They're so beautiful, the horses. Vinnie used to take us to Palm Beach. It was fun. A little outta my league tho."

Lorna listened to Doreen while staring at her back. "Have I told you in the last five minutes that your ass is second to none?"

Doreen responded by wiggling it.

Lorna shook her head and continued. "So, Alice is an artist. Works mostly in watercolor. Needs new inspiration. I like her. She sounds focused. She asked me what the time limit was on the cabin, and I told her there was none. She was curious to know if I was looking for longevity, and I told her it was purely subjective."

"Yeah, you don't want to hem anyone in, right?"

"No, there's no lease. For as long as it lasts. And I kind of hope these women move on to their future as artists. As long as they come here to create and grow."

Doreen turned around, drying her hands on a dishtowel. "Did you ask her what the nickname stood for?"

Lorna looked at Doreen and tossed the papers aside. She stood up to approach Doreen. "I'm sorry, but I think I have to kiss you because your mouth is just too divine. The nickname inquiry will have to wait."

Doreen responded by picking Lorna up by the ass and taking her over to the kitchen table. Lorna straddled Doreen around her waist with her legs.

The kitchen table contents were on the floor in ten seconds.

Luckily, the dishes were already in the sink.

The following day, Anya found Lorna and Doreen relaxing on the beach.

"Oh, hello, Misses."

Lorna looked up from her position on the beach lounge. "Hi. You going to join us for a little relaxation?"

"Oh, no Miss. I came to tell you there is someone in the lobby who is asking to see you. She did not, well, *would* not give me her name. Said she was an old, old friend of yours, had not seen you for many, many, years, from up north and wanted to surprise you."

Lorna's hackles rose immediately.

Doreen stopped reading her Harley Mechanics tome.

"Oh? What does she look like?"

Anya shrugged. "Like a woman, really."

"Okay, well."

Doreen said, "What's up, hon? Who do you think it is?"

Lorna felt her insides tingle. A squirm ran the course of her intestines.

It couldn't be.

"What did you tell her, Anya?"

"I told her you were getting to some relaxation at the beach with Miss Doreen. She asked me to tell her how to get to where the beach was, and I thought maybe I should tell you first. She was wearing, like high heels and a dress. So, I told her to sit in the lobby, and I brought her some lemonade. Then I came down here."

Doreen asked, "Do you think it's an old friend from school, maybe?"

"Yeah. From school."

Doreen cocked her head. She studied Lorna for a few moments then seemed to catch on. "Ah, shit."

"Yeah. Oh shit."

Anya said, "You want for me to tell her you are busy right now?"

Lorna stared out into the vast Atlantic. The crystalline white caps flowed carelessly towards the beach, the surf lapping quietly over the shells and debris. The sun warmed her shoulders, and her head was a little fuzzy from feeling so peaceful.

"No. I'll be right up." She felt Doreen's hand on her arm. The warmth of it made her feel good, safe.

She knew she would not have to explain.

She leaned down and kissed Doreen gently on the lips, told her she had this covered in no uncertain terms with her eyes, then turned to go up to the motel.

When she entered the lobby and saw her from behind, she automatically straightened her shoulders. What she saw when she came around to the front of the woman was nothing short of surprising. Yes, the same pale blue eyes greeted her, and yes, the same crooked smile. But the rest of her had matured beyond her age. She looked old and tired. Her hair, while tied back in a bun, appeared dry and un-styled.

"Hello, Lorna." The voice cut through her.

It startled her, bringing her back to those few years when nothing in the world mattered but their love. When her future had more possibilities than she could imagine. When it all came to a screeching halt that afternoon on the front steps with words spoken through a dark-webbed threshold.

Words that cut and eviscerated the purity of their love right out from underneath her.

Her throat went dry, the periphery of the room began to vignette.

She whispered, "Jeanie."

-The End-

Post Script- A Note to Readers

Pagodaville is far from over. In fact, it's just the beginning! Now that you've met Lorna and her gang of misfits, get ready for the next installment:

The Ladies of Pagodaville.

Meet musician PK Todd, writer Sam Harper, illustrator Gloria 'Lindy' Sutton, and artist Alice 'Lucky' Punston.

They will teach each other, through their conflicts and successes in life, how to grow as individuals and as a family and that love, indeed, does conquer most, if not all, of life's errant pitches.

Throw in Sam's loveable 10-year old mutt named Bullseye (AKA Bean), a few unexpected visitations to the motel, and a radical piece of history in 1981 that changed the lives of gay people everywhere.

Come, let's get lost!

About the Author

Ellen Bennett currently resides in West Michigan. This is her first published work. She is a Medical Massage Practitioner by trade, an amateur photographer and musician, and dabbles in community theater. You may read more about Ellen on the following web page:www.smilingdogpublicationsllc.com.

Pagodaville